What About Goldfish?

DATE DUE

JUN 08 '06			

GAYLORD 234   PRINTED IN U.S.A.

What About My Goldfish?

by Pamela D. Greenwood
Illustrated by Jennifer Plecas

Clarion Books
New York

Clarion Books
a Houghton Mifflin Company imprint
215 Park Avenue South, New York, NY 10003
Text copyright © 1993 by Pamela Greenwood
Illustrations copyright © 1993 by Jennifer Plecas

Printed in the U.S.A.

Book design by Sylvia Frezzolini

Library of Congress Cataloging-in-Publication Data
Greenwood, Pamela D.
    What about my goldfish? / by Pamela D. Greenwood ;
illustrated by Jennifer Plecas.
        p.   cm.
Summary: Jamie worries about moving to another city, but with
the help of his dog and pet goldfish, he adjusts to his new home.
    ISBN 0-395-64337-6
    [1. Moving, Household—Fiction.   2. Pets—Fiction.]
I. Plecas, Jennifer, ill.   II. Title.
PZ7.G85326Wh   1993   92-11281
[E]—dc20   CIP
                                                     AC

BP   10   9   8   7   6   5   4   3   2   1

Contents

CHAPTER 1

We're Moving

We're moving.
Dad got a new job.
Mom told me today.
I went out to the porch and hugged my dog.
Mom followed me.

"What if Freckles won't leave home?" I asked.

"Her home is with us," Mom said.

"What if we can't find her when it's time to move?"

"Don't worry, Jamie. We won't leave without her."

I took Freckles for a walk through our neighborhood.

I didn't want her to forget it.

The next day I told my teacher we were going
to move.

"We'll miss you, Jamie." Ms. Dillow put her hand
on my shoulder. "When are you moving?"

"Dad said we have to sell our house first."

Maybe no one will buy it, I thought.

I told my friends at recess.

"Where?" "Why?" "When?" they asked.

"Can we still be friends?" asked Joe.

"I think so," I answered.

"Can I have your goldfish?" Terry asked. "The water will spill out if you try to move them."

Mom fixed apple slices for my after-school snack.

"What about my goldfish?" I asked.

"What about them?" Mom said.

"Freckles will miss them," I said. "She likes to watch Skunk and Merlin play together when I'm at school."

"We'll take them with us," Mom said.

"Won't the water spill?"

"We'll put them in a big jar. With a lid."

"Oh," I said. "Freckles will be glad."

I took a bite of apple.

"What about Joe?"

Mom laughed. "We can't take *him* with us."

"Can we still be friends?"

"You can always keep your friends."

CHAPTER 2

Pet Day, Last Day

It was Pet Day at school. And my last day at Jackson Elementary.

We took turns telling about our pets.

"Freckles didn't sleep last night," I said. "She wonders if there will be anyone to play with in our new neighborhood."

Ms. Dillow smiled at Freckles. "She'll make new friends when you take her for walks."

Mom came to school for my going-away party. She took pictures.

I had brought chocolate chip cookies to share.

When I gave out the cookies, I gave out postcards with my new address on them.

I wanted everyone to write to me.

"Can you come back for my birthday party?"
Joe asked.

I looked at Mom. "You can send a birthday
card," she said.

"Are you sure you're taking your goldfish?"
Terry asked. "I'll give them a good home if you
change your mind."

"I'm sure," I said.

CHAPTER 3

On Our Way

The movers arrived before breakfast.

I carried the box marked SPECIAL STUFF to our car. It had my favorite toys, my red shirt, and two new books. It had a chew stick for Freckles.

Then I followed the movers to make sure they got all the other boxes.

Freckles barked and ran in and out between their legs.

Dad said, "I'd better find a quiet spot for her."

Finally, the house was empty.

It didn't look like our house anymore.

I went outside.

I called Freckles.

No answer.

"Dad," I said, "I can't find Freckles."

"In a minute, Jamie," he said in an I-don't-hear-you voice.

He was signing papers for the movers.

I ran inside.

"Mom, we can't move," I shouted.

"I know it's not easy," Mom said, "but we—"

"Freckles is gone," I said. "You said we wouldn't leave without her."

"Freckles won't let us leave without her." Dad was standing in the doorway. "Come into the garage."

Freckles was curled up in the back seat of the car.

"She's ready to go, and so are we," Dad said.

I climbed into the back seat with Freckles.

I nuzzled my face into her neck.

She licked some tears off my cheeks.

Mom handed me the goldfish jar. I put it on the floor between my feet.

Dad backed out of the garage.

"Where's the picture of our new house?"
I asked.

Mom took it from her purse.

I held it tightly.

I looked at the big tree just outside my
new room.

"This will be fun to climb," I said.

I leaned my head against the seat.

The water in the fish jar sloshed as we turned a corner.

"Are we almost there?" I asked.

CHAPTER 4

Moving In

It took three days to get to our new house.

When Dad finally stopped the car at our new front door, I kicked my feet up and down to wake them up.

"Let's unload the car," he said.

I got my sleeping bag. Mom and Dad got theirs.
"The movers should get here tomorrow,"
Mom said.

She made hot chocolate with the cocoa mix she
had brought along.

I walked around. My footsteps echoed through
the empty house.

I found my room.

The leaves of the climbing tree whispered
against the window. It was dark outside.

I brought my sleeping bag back downstairs.
"This is a noisy house," I said. "Let's all sleep in
the living room. Freckles doesn't know her way
around yet."
"Good idea," Dad agreed.

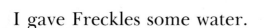

I gave Freckles some water.

I blew on my cocoa until it was cool enough to sip.

I looked around the living room.

"What about my goldfish? Where are they?"

"In the kitchen," Mom said.

I put them next to my sleeping bag. Freckles curled up at my feet.

"Good night, Merlin," I said. "Good night, Skunk. Sleep tight, Freckles."

Freckles was already asleep.

CHAPTER 5

No Dogs in Class

My new teacher called me Jimmy three times. She made me stay in at recess to copy the spelling list. She didn't want to hear about Pet Day.

After school, I checked the mailbox.

I got a postcard from Joe.

"Remember Freckles at Pet Day?" he wrote. "She ate my chocolate chip cookie. From, Joe. P.S. How is your new school?"

"It stinks," I said.

"What?" Mom asked.

"My new school stinks."

"Why?"

"I asked Mrs. Chapman if Freckles could visit my school. 'No dogs in class,' she said. What can I tell Freckles?"

"You'll think of something," Mom said.

I worked on my spelling words.
Then I took Freckles out to play fetch.
I threw the ball and she chased it.
She brought it back.
"Sorry you can't go to school," I told her.
I threw the ball again.
What about my goldfish? I thought. If Skunk and Merlin go to school, they can tell Freckles about it.

Mrs. Chapman said it would be okay to bring my goldfish for show-and-tell.

Mom and I put the goldfish back in the jar.

"Don't worry," I told them. "You're not moving again."

Mom drove me to school because the jar was too heavy to carry.

When Mrs. Chapman called on me, I put the goldfish jar on her desk and stood behind it.

"How old are they?" Jill asked.

"Why aren't they gold?" asked Tim.

"They're almost two," I said.

"Why aren't they gold if they're *gold*fish?"
Tim repeated.

"Goldfish are a kind of fish, not a color,"
I told him.

"Sure," he said, like he didn't believe me.

"Why did you name them Skunk and Merlin?"
Nate asked.

"Skunk is black and white," I said. "And Merlin,
well, Merlin disappeared a lot when I first got
him. He still likes to hide."

"So what?" asked Tim.

"Merlin is a magician's name," I answered. "Magicians can make themselves disappear."

I wish *you* would disappear, I thought. You ask too many questions.

After school, I was putting the goldfish jar in the car.

Tim walked by. "I like your black and white and orange fish," he said.

"Thanks," I said.

Maybe Tim's not so bad, I thought. Maybe he just wants to learn about goldfish.

CHAPTER 6

The Pond

The next day Tim and I walked home from school together.

I told him about Freckles.

"I can't have a dog," he said. "My sister is allergic."

Tim told me about the birthday party Peter had last Friday.

"Susan's party is Saturday," he said. "Are you going?"

I shook my head.

When I got home, I told Mom about the parties. "Everyone was invited. Everyone but me."

"When they get to know you better," Mom said, "then you'll be invited too."

"I want to have a birthday party," I said. "When you ask kids to your party, then they ask you to theirs."

"But it's not your birthday," Mom said.

"My birthday isn't till summer. Nobody will ask me to a party for the rest of the year."

Freckles and I went outside.

Dad was cleaning the pond in our backyard.

Beside him was a box of lily pads he'd bought at the store. I helped him put them into the water.

"Know what else this pond needs?" he asked.

"Goldfish," I answered.

"Know where I can get some big, healthy goldfish?"

"At the store," I said.

Dad added more water to the pond with the hose.

"What about your goldfish?" he asked.

"Skunk and Merlin?" My voice was so loud Freckles barked. "Not Skunk and Merlin. It's a big pond. They'll get lonely out here."

"It could be a new adventure for them," Dad said. "Think about it, Jamie."

Dad took his tools to the garage.

Freckles and I stretched out by the pond. The grass tickled right through my shirt. We looked into the water.

Merlin would have new places to hide under the lily pads. Skunk could race around.

"Maybe they wouldn't be lonely if they had new friends," I told Freckles.

Then I got an idea.

"I don't have to have a *birthday* party. I can have a *pond* party."

I ran inside to tell Mom about it.

"I'll ask everyone to bring a goldfish instead of a present. Skunk and Merlin will be waiting in the pond. They'll make lots of new friends. I will too."

"Sounds great," Mom said.

I got the construction paper. I made fish-shaped invitations. Orange and blue and white and green ones. I made Tim's green.

CHAPTER 7

A Party

The morning of the party Dad and I put Skunk and Merlin back into the jar. We took them to the pond.

"Are you sure they'll like it?" I asked.

"I'm sure," Dad said.

I put Merlin in the pond. He hid under the nearest lily pad.

Then Skunk. He raced around just like I thought he would.

Nate arrived first. Then Tim and Jill. Soon my whole class was there.

One by one the new fish joined Skunk and Merlin in the pond.

I looked at the new fish. Then I looked
at my new friends.

Skunk and Merlin must be glad, I
thought.

We played pin-the-fins on a giant fish.
We played a hop-in-a-sack relay.
We ate tuna fish sandwiches.

"We'll invite Jamie over to play," Jill's mother
said to Mom when she came to get Jill.
  "Nate's having a birthday party next week," his
dad said. "We'd like Jamie to come."
  I smiled at Mom. She smiled back.

Tim stayed after everyone else had gone.
His mother had to work late.

"It's safe out here for Freckles now," Dad said.
He let her out of the house.

Tim and I played fetch with Freckles.

"When I bought your goldfish, my mother let
me buy one for myself," Tim said after he threw
the ball.

"Is it gold?" I asked.

Tim laughed and shook his head. "It's black
and white like Skunk."

"Does it have a name yet?" I asked.

"Spot," Tim said.

Freckles took the ball to Tim.

"I wish Spot could play fetch," he said.

"Freckles likes you," I said. "You can play fetch with her anytime."

Then we sat by the pond.

I let Tim feed the fish.

I showed him how to crumble the flakes between his fingers.

"You know a lot about goldfish," he said.

We heard his mother drive up. Mom and Dad went to the car to meet her.

"Maybe you can come over and help me
with Spot," Tim said.

I grinned. "Let's ask." And we ran to
the car together.

The
Forensic
Anthropologist

by Diane Yancey

LUCENT BOOKS
An imprint of Thomson Gale, a part of The Thomson Corporation

THOMSON
GALE

Detroit • New York • San Francisco • San Diego • New Haven, Conn. • Waterville, Maine • London • Munich

Acknowledgement

We would like to express our sincere gratitude to forensic anthropologist Madeleine Hinkes for her technical expertise which proved invaluable in the production of Lucent's *Crime Scene Investigations: The Forensic Anthropologist.*

© 2006 Thomson Gale, a part of The Thomson Corporation.

Thomson and Star Logo are trademarks and Gale and Lucent Books are registered trademarks used herein under license.

For more information, contact
Lucent Books
27500 Drake Rd.
Farmington Hills, MI 48331-3535
Or you can visit our Internet site at http://www.gale.com

LIBRARY OF CONGRESS CATALOGING-IN-PUBLICATION DATA

Yancey, Diane.
  The forensic anthropologist / by Diane Yancey.
      p. cm. — (Crime scene investigations)
  Includes bibliographical references and index.
  ISBN 1-59018-618-4 (hard cover : alk. paper) 1. Forensic anthropology—Juvenile literature. 2. Forensic osteology—Juvenile literature. I. Title. II. Series: Crime scene investigations series.
  GN69.8.Y36 2006
  614'.17—dc22
                                                          2005030519

Printed in the United States of America

Contents

Foreword

The popularity of crime scene and investigative crime shows on television has come as a surprise to many who work in the field. The main surprise is the concept that crime scene analysts are the true crime solvers, when in truth, it takes dozens of people, doing many different jobs, to solve a crime. Often, the crime scene analyst's contribution is a small one. One Minnesota forensic scientist says that the public "has gotten the wrong idea. Because I work in a lab similar to the ones on *CSI,* people seem to think I'm solving crimes left and right—just me and my microscope. They don't believe me when I tell them that it's the investigators that are solving crimes, not me."

Crime scene analysts do have an important role to play, however. Science has rapidly added a whole new dimension to gathering and assessing evidence. Modern crime labs can match a hair of a murder suspect to one found on a murder victim, for example, or recover a latent fingerprint from a threatening letter, or use a powerful microscope to match tool marks made during the wiring of an explosive device to a tool in a suspect's possession.

Probably the most exciting of the forensic scientist's tools is DNA analysis. DNA can be found in just one drop of blood, a dribble of saliva on a toothbrush, or even the residue from a fingerprint. Some DNA analysis techniques enable scientists to tell with certainty, for example, whether a drop of blood on a suspect's shirt is that of a murder victim.

While these exciting techniques are now an essential part of many investigations, they cannot solve crimes alone. "DNA doesn't come with a name and address on it," says the Minnesota forensic scientist. "It's great if you have someone in custody to match the sample to, but otherwise, it doesn't help. That's the investigator's job. We can have all the great DNA evidence in the world, and without a suspect, it will just sit on the shelf. We've all seen cases with very little forensic evidence get solved by the resourcefulness of a detective."

While forensic specialists get the most media attention today, the work of detectives still forms the core of most criminal investigations. Their job, in many ways, has changed little over the years. Most cases are still solved through the persistence and determination of a criminal detective whose work may be anything but glamorous. Many cases require routine, even mind-numbing tasks. After the July 2005 bombings in London, for example, police officers sat in front of video players watching thousands of hours of closed-circuit television tape from security cameras throughout the city, and as a result were able to get the first images of the bombers.

The Lucent Books Crime Scene Investigations series explores the variety of ways crimes are solved. Titles cover particular crimes such as murder, specific cases such as the killing of three civil rights workers in Mississippi, or the role specialists such as medical examiners play in solving crimes. Each title in the series demonstrates the ways a crime may be solved, from the various applications of forensic science and technology to the reasoning of investigators. Sidebars examine both the limits and possibilities of the new technologies and present crime statistics, career information, and step-by-step explanations of scientific and legal processes.

The Crime Scene Investigations series strives to be both informative and realistic about how members of law enforcement—criminal investigators, forensic scientists, and others—solve crimes, for it is essential that student researchers understand that crime solving is rarely quick or easy. Many factors—from a detective's dogged pursuit of one tenuous lead to a suspect's careless mistakes to sheer luck to complex calculations computed in the lab—are all part of crime solving today.

The Bone Experts

When George and Marie DeLeon spotted a human skull lying beside a country road near San Antonio, Texas, in December 2004, they could scarcely believe their eyes. George stopped the car and called the police, who initiated a search, but no other bones were found.

The skull was taken to the county crime lab, where the medical examiner was unable to match it to a missing person. Unwilling to give up, however, he contacted forensic anthropologist Harrell Gill-King. A forensic anthropologist is an individual who examines skeletal or badly decomposed remains to provide identification and/or analysis of injuries in order to help solve crimes, and Gill-King is one of the best. The director of the Laboratory of Forensic Anthropology and Human Identification at the University of North Texas, he had helped identify victims of the Oklahoma City bombing in 1995, the 9/11 terrorist attacks in 2001, and the *Columbia* space shuttle disaster in 2003. He was willing to lend a hand in this case because of both his compassion for victims and his unquenchable desire to learn more about bones. "Because of the different things we see and are asked to find, this line of work is an ongoing education," Gill-King observes. "We're always learning something new, and that something might make our next case easier."[1]

It did not take Gill-King long to get important information from the skull. The size and delicacy told him it was the skull of a female, and the teeth indicated the victim had been between eleven and fourteen years old. The shape of the eye sockets and other details suggested she was white or Hispanic. The police checked databases for missing white and Hispanic

In 2003 a forensic anthropologist in Guatemala uses a brush to remove dirt from the skull of a political prisoner murdered by the government nearly forty years before.

girls and found that a twelve-year-old runaway named Rosa Sandoval had lived just 7 miles (11.26m) from where the skull had been found. DNA from a tooth was consistent with DNA taken from Sandoval's parents. The skull finally had a name and an identity. How Rosa died was still a mystery, but Gill-King took satisfaction from knowing that her parents did not have to continue wondering where she was.

An Underrated Specialty

In helping to solve cases like the Sandoval death, forensic anthropologists like Gill-King use skills and techniques that were unknown to the general public until the 1990s. Forensic anthropology was formally recognized by the scientific community in 1972, when the American Academy of Forensic Sciences created a Physical Anthropology Section. This department is concerned with the interests, activities, education, and expertise of forensic anthropologists. Before that time, the subject was seen as a subbranch of anatomy, and anthropologists focused primarily on studying ancient humans. Many even felt that lending their skills to the police upon request was inap-

Dr. Aleš Hrdlička, curator of physical anthropology at the Smithsonian, assisted the FBI in thirty-seven criminal cases.

propriate and demeaning to their professional position.

Anthropologists who worked at the Smithsonian Institution's National Museum of Natural History in Washington, D.C., played a significant role in changing the notion that anthropology and crime should not mix. The prestigious museum, with its collection of ancient bones, sits just across the street from the headquarters of the Federal Bureau of Investigation (FBI). In 1938, while trying to determine whether a set of skeletal remains was human, FBI director J. Edgar Hoover asked Aleš Hrdlička, the museum's curator of physical anthropology, to look at the bones and give an opinion. Hrdlička, agreed, and went on to help the FBI with at least thirty-seven cases before his death in 1943.

Clyde Snow is one of the most famous forensic anthropologists in the world.

T. Dale Stewart, who succeeded Hrdlička, as curator in 1942, was more open in his relationship with the FBI. During his twenty-year tenure, he consulted on more than 167 cases, and he regularly testified as an expert witness in murder trials, something that his predecessor had refused to do. After his retirement, Stewart published the first textbook for forensic anthropologists, *Essentials of Forensic Anthropology*, in 1979.

By the time J. Lawrence Angel became curator of physical anthropology at the Smithsonian in 1962, the FBI had begun to fully appreciate the role of physical anthropologists as forensic experts. The bureau regularly turned to Angel as its primary authority in identifying unknown bones. He worked on 646 cases during a fifteen-year period. By that time, other anthropologists in the United States had become fascinated with crime solving. Three of them—William Maples, Clyde Snow, and William Bass III—came to be recognized as leaders in the world of forensic science.

Leaders in the World of Forensics

William Maples earned his PhD in anthropology from the University of Texas in 1967 and identified his first set of remains in 1972. As word of his expertise spread, his caseload of forensic work became so heavy that he outgrew the facilities of the Florida Museum of Natural History, located at the University of Florida in Gainesville, where he served as curator. In 1991 he founded the C.A. Pound Human Identification Laboratory at the university. The lab was (and still is) considered one of the most innovative in the United States, and Maples received calls for help in solving crimes from all over the world. During his career, he worked on such high-profile cases as identifying the true cause of death of President Zachary Taylor, identifying the remains of Spanish explorer Francisco Pizarro, and analyzing the bones of Joseph Merrick, the "Elephant Man."

Before the field of forensic anthropology was born, anthropology was associated primarily with the discovery of ancient remains, such as this 4-million-year-old hominid jawbone.

Clyde Snow, perhaps the most famous forensic anthropologist in the world, earned his PhD in anthropology from the University of Arizona in 1967. By then, he was already adept at reading bones because he had spent years studying airplane crashes for the Federal Aviation Administration in an attempt to improve airline safety.

In the 1980s Snow gained fame for exhuming mass graves in Argentina to identify civilians who had been killed by government death squads during a recent war. He later went on to exhume and identify victims of human rights abuse in Guatemala, Ethiopia, the Philippines, and Croatia. "Of all the forms of murder, none is more monstrous than that committed by a state against its own citizens,"[2] he says.

The Anthropologist and the Sausage Maker

The belief that it was unprofessional for anthropologists to testify in court was first tested by George Dorsey in 1899. Dorsey, the curator of physical anthropology at the Field Museum of Natural History in Chicago, was asked by police to look at tiny bone fragments believed to be the remains of Louisa Leutgert, wife of Chicago sausage maker Adolph Leutgert. Louisa had disappeared after a fight with her husband, and bones, a wedding ring, a steel corset stay, and a false tooth had been recovered from a cooking vat and a pile of ashes in the Leutgert factory. The bones were small enough to fit into a tablespoon, and a doctor had testified that it was impossible to tell whether they were animal or human. Dorsey, however, took the stand and identified them as a piece of the metacarpal bone from the hand, a piece of a rib, a small piece of a phalanx, or toe bone, and the sesamoid bone from the joint of the big toe.

Adolph Leutgert was convicted and sentenced to life in prison based on Dorsey's testimony, but the anthropologist was attacked by his colleagues for demeaning himself by "performing" at a trial. He was also criticized for challenging a medical doctor's opinion. Despite Dorsey's personal sufferings, his testimony paved the way for later anthropologists who help the police bring criminals to justice.

William Bass completed his PhD in anthropology at the University of Pennsylvania in 1961. In 1977, when he miscalculated the age of a hundred-year-old skeleton that had been dug out of a Civil War graveyard in Tennessee, he realized he had much more to learn about how the human body changes after death. Motivated by his mistake, Bass founded the University of Tennessee's Forensic Anthropology Facility in 1980. The facility's sole purpose is to allow scientists to study human decomposition under as many conditions as possible.

The Body Farm, as it came to be called, became famous for the array of decomposing corpses that littered its grounds, and Bass became legendary for his contributions to forensic science. Anthropologist Emily Craig writes, "Until Dr. Bass came along, forensic scientists who were asked to establish time since death of a badly decomposed or skeletonized body had to rely upon guesswork and experience. . . . Now, thanks to Dr. Bass's pioneering work, we have documented scientific studies to back up our hunches."[3]

Those Who Follow

Emily Craig and Harrell Gill-King are two bone experts who have benefited from the work of early forensic anthropologists such as Snow, Maples, and Bass. Since there are only about forty-five board-certified forensic anthropologists in the world today, they and their colleagues are busy individuals. Some are involved in full-time crime solving, working in conjunction with police, medical examiners, and other forensic experts. Others also work as museum curators and professors at universities, where they focus on ancient bones dug from archaeological sites. What they learn from ancient skeletons provides them with data that can be applied to bones found in modern times.

When they are called in to help solve crimes, they are exposed to conditions that many would consider gruesome and disturbing. The victims have usually suffered violent deaths, and their bodies are reduced to rotting tissue and greasy bones. The places they lie in are often difficult to access, swarming with flies, and reeking with the foul odor of decay.

For forensic anthropologists, however, the human body is endlessly fascinating, and the rewards of identifying victims and bringing killers to justice are much greater than any temporary discomfort they may endure. As forensic anthropologist Mary H. Manhein observes, "If you don't mind low pay, night and weekend work, treacherous recovery sites, snakes, mosquitoes, and poison ivy, then a career in forensic anthropology . . . could give you amazing job satisfaction."[4]

CHAPTER 1

Recovering the Bones

Although forensic anthropologists often work in the lab or classroom, they are also respected participants at crime scenes. This is because most anthropologists are skilled at fieldwork, having learned to exhume graves in order to study ancient humans. Their knowledge of burial sites and their ability to carefully unearth remains makes them invaluable in forensics because their painstaking work allows them to interpret crime scenes more precisely than other experts might. Authors Douglas Ubelaker and Henry Scammell explain:

> Experienced forensic anthropologists have examined thousands of bones from all time periods and from all over the world. . . . They know what happens to a skeleton after the passage of a month, a decade, a century, two thousand years. . . . They can distinguish between evidence of murder and the results of a dog passing by and helping himself to lunch.[5]

At the Crime Scene

A crime scene can be extremely complex territory, involving the place where a victim dies, the place where the body is deposited, and any other places where evidence may be found. Bone experts, however, focus on the place where human remains lie. This may be inside an automobile or on a rocky mountainside. It may be in a well, an old refrigerator, or a long-forgotten box in an attic. In a 2003 case in Brownwood, Texas, it was the crawl space of a house owned by a family that had lived there for several years. While remodeling, the family had

A forensic expert works painstakingly to remove the dirt surrounding the remains of a genocide victim in Bosnia.

Becoming a Forensic Anthropologist

Job Description:
Forensic anthropologists help identify unknown bodies or body parts and skeletal remains, providing facts such as estimated time since death and determination of ante-, peri- and postmortem trauma. Work is carried out both in the lab and in the field. The work involves exposure to potentially dangerous and disturbing situations. Most work is part-time, or on an as-needed basis.

Education:
Aspiring forensic anthropologists must first earn a Bachelor of Arts degree (BA) in anthropology from a four-year college, then a Master of Arts (MA) degree in anthropology, followed by a PhD in anthropology.

A forensic scientist examines a human bone discovered at a dump in Bosnia.

Qualifications:
Once their education is completed, forensic anthropologists should achieve board certification by the American Board of Forensic Anthropology.

Salary:
$40,000 to $100,000 annually.

entered the space and found the bodies of three babies hidden in a trash bag. No one could tell exactly when the babies had been placed there, or by whom, and the case is still under investigation. Dallas forensic pathologist Linda Norton, a highly regarded expert on infant deaths, believes the most likely suspect is someone who once lived in the house, "or someone connected to someone who lived in the house."[6]

An indoor crime scene is relatively easy to examine because the remains have usually been protected by a roof and walls. Sometimes, however, the site can be very confined. Such was the case in 1991, when a termite inspector found a skeleton under the enclosed front porch of a home in southeast Louisiana. Mary Manhein had to crawl on her stomach under the dark porch to examine the remains by flashlight. She remembers "The hole was just big enough for me to squeeze through and proved a little too close for my 6-foot, 2-inch assistant. His claustrophobia prevented him from lingering long at the entryway."[7]

In the case of a house or building fire, cleanliness and order disappear. Forensic anthropologists often have to carefully sift through layers of ash and debris to find the remains. Reading the scene is extremely difficult, and they have to rely on subtle clues even to get their bearings in a room. For example, metal feet may mark where chairs or tables stood, while metal coat hangers can define closets. In *Death's Acre*, Bill Bass and Jon Jefferson note, "Those buttons, snaps, hooks and eyes, brass rivets and zippers embedded in a heap of ashes? Easy: a chest of drawers once crammed with shirts and brassieres and blue jeans. That mound of broken glass and porcelain beside a charred chandelier? It was once the china cabinet in the dining room."[8]

Processing the Crime Scene

Except for fire scenes, outdoor crime scenes are usually more time consuming to examine than indoor ones, in part because their boundaries are more difficult to define. Investigators also have to determine whether remains are part of a historic or prehistoric burial site or the result of a more recent death. Construction crews frequently unearth ancient skeletons during road or housing excavations. Bone experts know that if a skeleton shows signs of having been embalmed or is accompanied by coffin nails or arrow points, it usually represents a death from the distant past. If this is the case, the bones are collected and transported to a more protected resting place.

Before beginning work on a mass grave in Argentina, a team of forensic anthropologists divided the site into a grid in order to precisely map the location of unearthed remains.

If the remains prove to be recent, the immediate vicinity is cordoned off with yellow tape so that curious bystanders cannot disturb anything. This perimeter can be expanded if evidence is later found outside that boundary. Then the scene is divided into strips, grids, or zones, and carefully searched. Anthropologists rely on archeological recovery techniques to expose a completely buried body before lifting it from the ground. Using small tools such as hand trowels, dental picks, and paintbrushes, they remove dirt without damaging the bones or dislodging trace evidence.

Field Equipment

Picks and paintbrushes are not the only equipment anthropologists need to properly process a site. Bass and Jefferson write, "The anthropology department [of the University of Tennessee] . . . had a pickup truck, which we kept loaded at all times with the equipment we'd need in the field—shovels and trowels for digging; wire-mesh screens for sifting small bones and bone fragments from dirt; three body bags for transporting corpses in the back of the truck."[9]

Recovery kits also include boots, overalls, latex gloves, safety glasses, and dust masks to protect investigators from

A forensic specialist uses a trowel and a paintbrush to remove dirt from bones discovered in a mass grave in Iraq.

disease-causing organisms that are present when bodies decompose. Paper bags, used to hold evidence such as bullet casings and cigarette butts, are vital. Plastic bags are seldom used in recovery, because they create an airless environment and increase the chance of mildew or further decomposition.

Working Methodically

Red or orange survey flags are brought along to mark the location of each bone or piece of evidence, and at least two cameras are included so that every detail can be recorded. At each recovery site, a photographer is assigned to take pictures from the moment the team arrives until the last person leaves. This is because the scene will change over time, and no one can predict which details will be an important reference point in the future. "Shoot your way in, and shoot your way out," says Harold Nye, a former Kansas law enforcement officer skilled in crime scene investigation.

> When you arrive at the scene and get out of your car, take a picture of the house or the car or whatever the scene is. As you walk closer, take some more. Take pictures of the ground before you walk on it; take pictures of who's there; pictures of what kind of shoes officers at the scene are wearing. Take pictures of the body before you move it or even touch it.[10]

Working slowly and methodically is important in any investigation. Emily Craig says,

> When I'm working a crime scene . . . I continually have to remind myself and everyone else to slow down. After all, the victims are already dead. . . . Despite the natural human reaction to respect the dead by removing and cleaning up their bodies as soon as possible, we actually show them more respect by leaving them where they are and documenting the evidence that can help us discover

how they died. Once you've moved a piece of evidence at a crime scene, that's it. You can never put it back.[11]

Piece by Piece

After photos are taken, the body or skeleton is carefully transferred onto a sheet, then zipped into a body bag. Any loose bones are carefully picked up, packaged, and labeled.

Crucial Information

Anthropologist Emily Craig knows the importance of crime scene analysis. In Teasing Secrets from the Dead, *she recalls early visits to crime scenes while a student at the Body Farm.*

We never heard about "fresh" bodies—that was a job for the pathologist. But if they found decomposing remains, unassociated body parts, or bones, they'd call in the anthropologists. We'd rush to the scene—perhaps a farmhouse with two smoking corpses or maybe a back-alley apartment with a cache of bones hidden under the floorboards. . . .

Here is where I learned how crucial is the information gleaned from the scene. Sure, lab analysis was vitally important, but every investigator starts with the crime scene—if only you know how to look. On one very early case, I, the novice, saw nothing out of the ordinary until [a] fellow student . . . pointed out that the charred body in the car was covered with burned maggots. This was irrefutable evidence that the man, and his car, had been torched well after he had started to decompose.

In another case, the sheriff took me aside and told me that our murder suspect had just confessed to beating the victim to death with a golf club. I realized how close I might have come to disregarding the broken putter we'd just found in our search through a roadside dump for scattered bones.

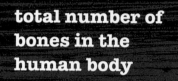

By the Numbers

206

total number of bones in the human body

The process is often made more difficult by the location of the body. The skeleton of one murder victim was found at the bottom of a well, so the anthropologist had to be lowered on ropes, wearing a special breathing apparatus, to retrieve it. Another skeleton was found deep inside a coal mine, where the recovery team had to slither on their stomachs and maneuver in close quarters to bag the body, then drag the body bag behind them for hundreds of yards until they reached a more open area. In a third instance, the remains of an industrial worker had to be retrieved from between two large elevated storage tanks, where he had fallen during a fire in the plant. Manhein was one of the recovery crew who scaled the heights of a scaffold to get to the body. High above the ground she was overcome with poisonous fumes and had to be revived before the recovery could be completed. "'Field recovery' . . . took on a new meaning for me [after that],"[12] she remembers.

No matter where the retrieval process takes place, investigators must exercise extreme care so that trace evidence such as hair and fibers are collected. The ground under the bones is always carefully checked to be sure that no evidence—or even another body—is still hidden. Sometimes the underlying earth itself is collected for further inspection. At a crime scene in Massachusetts in 1985, Ubelaker, an anthropologist with the Smithsonian, obtained two huge chunks of earth containing roots, vines, dead shrubbery, and human bones. By examining the earth, including root systems that had grown through the victim's clothing and bones, Ubelaker was able to determine how much time had passed since death as well as the trajectory of a bullet found in the victim's remains.

Complications

An important part of every search is that made for bones that have been covered by falling leaves, carried off by animals, or washed away by rain. The study of how these and other out-side factors affect bodies after death is known as taphonomy. To be successful in crime scene work, a bone expert has to be an expert in taphonomy.

Bass and Jefferson note,

Taphonomy—the arrangement or relative position of the human remains, artifacts, and natural elements like earth, leaves, and insect casings—is one of the most crucial sources of information to a forensic anthropologist at a crime scene. . . . Are the bones within the clothing, or beside it? Is there a wasp nest in the skull, or a tree seedling growing up through the rib cage? All these things, and many more, are important pieces of the taphonomic puzzle; they can shed a lot of light on when or how someone died.[13]

In addition to the bones she has discovered, an Argentinean forensic specialist recovers a ball of mud she suspects might contain trace evidence such as hair and fibers.

Blow Fly Life Cycle

10 days

several hours

Adult
Within hours of a human's death, adult blow flies land on the corpse and begin feeding.

Pupae
The larval bodies change to adult flies, which mate on emergence from pupa.

Eggs
Flies lay eggs in clumps of up to 300.

4 days

1 day

Pre-pupa
The larvae migrate away from the corpse seeking a pupation site usually in the soil around the corpse.

Larvae
Eggs hatch and larvae feed on fluids oozing from the corpse; they migrate into the body through wounds; continue feeding, grow larger, and shed their skin.

4 days

Animal activity plays a significant role in taphonomy. If a body is left uncovered or buried in a shallow grave, the odors it emits as it begins to decompose immediately attract scavengers, including dogs, coyotes, rodents, wolves, and vultures. These animals eat the tissue, gnaw on the bones, and drag portions of the remains away to their nests, burrows, or dens.

To find scattered evidence, examiners begin at the point where the majority of the remains lie, and then methodically work outward. Particular attention is paid to trails formed by scavengers, since bones can be dropped along these almost-invisible paths. Animal droppings on the trails may hold undigested bones and missing teeth. Forensic anthropologist Roxana Ferllini writes, "By recovering the appropriate droppings, or 'scats,' they may be examined to recover the missing teeth, which are then compared to dental records. This search may not always be successful, but it has proved positive on several occasions."[14]

Water also has an impact on taphonomy. If a body is left on a steep slope, heavy rain may wash bones and other evidence down the hill. Rain can splatter dirt on bones, camouflaging them and sometimes covering them up entirely. If a body is dumped in a stream or river, bones are often carried downstream by the current. Experienced anthropologists know they must take all these factors into consideration when conducting a search.

Time of Death

Anthropologists investigate the crime scene not only to find hidden evidence, but also to try to determine how much time has passed since death occurred, called the postmortem interval. Skeletal remains can never reveal the exact moment a victim died, but a study of factors such as weather, plant growth, and insect activity can provide some information to help anthropologists determine how long a body has been at a scene.

Weather has a direct effect on how quickly a corpse decomposes, so it must be considered when determining time of death. Because insects and bacteria prefer warm, moist conditions, hot, humid days produce the fastest decomposition. Thus, remains found in regions with warm temperatures and high humidity may be badly decomposed after only two weeks. Extreme cold slows decomposition: In frozen climates bodies often show no signs of decay for months. Extremely dry conditions may shrivel and mummify a body before decomposition can take place. In the case of seven-year-old Danielle van Dam, who was murdered in Southern California in February 2002, the dry winds in the area where she lay partially mummified her body, slowed insect activity and decomposition, and made time of death extremely difficult to determine accurately.

Plants can also be good indicators of time of death. If the plants under the remains are relatively green, indicating they have recently been in the sun, the remains were deposited very recently. If the plants are yellow or dead, the remains have been lying on them at least a few weeks. If there are small trees growing up through the remains, they have been lying in one place for a season or more.

Flies, Beetles, and Other Bugs

Insect activity is another indicator of time of death. Within hours of death, flies and other insects arrive at a corpse and begin laying hundreds of eggs in wounds and other openings. When those eggs hatch, masses of larvae—also known as maggots—feed on the body as they progress through their life cycles. Anthropologists often work in conjunction with insect experts called forensic entomologists, who know the order in which different species invade a body after death and how long it takes for each to reproduce. They know that various insect species go through predictable life cycles and leave behind evidence of how long they have been present.

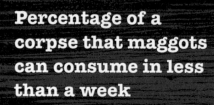

By the Numbers

60%

Percentage of a corpse that maggots can consume in less than a week

With their vast knowledge of insects, entomologists can sometimes estimate within a period of days when death occurred. For instance, in 1996 entomologist M. Lee Goff was asked to assist with the body of a marine found in a rain forest on Oahu, Hawaii. The corpse was badly decomposed, but when Goff inspected it he found the larvae of soldier flies. Their presence was fortunate, because in Hawaii, more than three hundred species of insects can infest a body from the time of death until it is completely decomposed, but only the life cycles of the most common have been studied thoroughly. The soldier fly is one such species.

Goff knew that soldier flies come to a body and lay their eggs about twenty days after death. The larvae he found were in the fifth instar (developmental stage), which meant they had been laid between nine and eleven days before. Adding the times together, he determined that death had occurred twenty-nine to thirty-one days before. Relying on Goff's expert opinion, military police interviewed two marines who had been seen with the victim thirty days before, and they confessed to the murder.

Dr. William Bass founded The Body Farm, where forensic specialists can study decomposing bodies.

A Simple Idea

No one has studied the postmortem interval in greater detail than the researchers at the Body Farm at the University of Tennessee. Over the years at this facility, more than three hundred donated corpses have been placed in car trunks, left in direct sunlight, covered with canvas and plastic, buried in mud, hung from scaffolds, locked into coffins, refrigerated in the dark, zipped into body bags, and submerged in water. Some are clothed. Some are naked. Some are embalmed.

As the bodies decompose and are exposed to the elements, insects, and small animals, students carefully record the changes they undergo. The purpose of the work is simple: to determine how long it takes for a body to decompose under specific conditions. If a body is ever found under similar conditions somewhere else in the world, this research will provide guidelines to help investigators judge how long it has been dead. Bass and Jefferson write, "The idea was simple: the implications—and the possible complications—were profound."[15]

Famous for its groundbreaking research, the Body Farm remains the only university facility of its kind in the world. Bass believes this is because the topic of death is often shunned in Western culture, so administrators are hesitant to support such research. He states, "By most cultural standards and values, such research could appear gruesome, disrespectful, even shocking."[16]

While some might consider bone research disrespectful, anthropologists always treat their subjects with the utmost respect, whether at the Body Farm, at a crime scene, or in the lab. They never forget that these were once living, breathing human beings with loved ones who cared about them. Thus, the bones are never tossed aside, played with, or made the object of humor. As William Maples once responded when asked if he had a nickname for the demonstration skeleton in his lab: "I call him the skeleton. It is my belief that every set of remains deserves a certain minimum of respect. We owe them that."[17]

CHAPTER 2

Reading the Bones

When bone experts are not in the field, they are in the laboratory. Forensic anthropology labs are usually part of state or federal crime labs, where men and women who specialize in firearms, tool marks, hairs and fibers, latent fingerprints, and DNA analysis work to find solutions to crimes. Author David Fisher writes, "The crime lab is that place where science meets murder. It's where the wonders of modern science and space-age technology are used to transform clues into hard evidence."[18]

Anthropologists in the lab often receive boxes or bags of bones from police or medical examiners elsewhere in the country, and are asked to gather as much information as possible from them. In such cases, the first question they always ask themselves is: Are these bones human? If the answer is yes, they go on to determine other factors, such as the sex, race, age, and height of the individual in question.

Human or Animal?

Similarities between animal and human bones often lead to confusion, and it takes the sharp eye of a knowledgeable expert to tell the difference. The FBI estimates that between 10 and 15 percent of the presumed human skeletal remains sent to it each year turn out to be those of animals.

When examining questionable bones, anthropologists first do a simple visual scan and assign each bone an identity, such as rib, leg bone, or jawbone. If the bone is a rib, they then must determine whether it is the correct size and weight to be human. If it is a piece of skull, they must compare it to a human skull to see if its contours and thickness are similar. In long

Forensic anthropologist Mary Manhein holds a human thigh bone as she teaches police detectives how to distinguish human from animal remains.

bones, they must look at the ends to determine whether the protuberances and the angles of the joints correspond to those of human arm and leg bones. Since humans walk upright on two legs, their leg bones are attached to the pelvis at a particular angle. This angle is distinctively different in animals that walk on four legs.

If the bones are so damaged that they cannot be definitively identified by sight, anthropologists look at them in cross-section under a microscope. Bones are not solid throughout; they are made up of a dense, hard outer layer called the cortex and an inner space filled with spongy material called cancellous tissue. In the cortex are osteons—channels through which blood vessels and nerve fibers run. In humans, the cortex is about one-quarter the total diameter of the bone, and the osteons are scattered randomly throughout the tissue. In animals, the cortex is thicker, about one-third the total diameter of the bone, and the osteons are lined up in rows that look like stacks of bricks when viewed under a microscope.

"A Watched Pot Never Boils"

Before they can examine partially decomposed bodies or bones with muscle, skin, or other tissue still attached, anthropologists must first clean them thoroughly. This cleaning process, called thermal maceration, is usually carried out by placing the remains in pots or vats filled with water, detergent, or chemicals and simmering them gently until all the tissue has fallen off. In the best-equipped labs, like the C.A. Pound Human Identification Laboratory, the vats are placed under large fume hoods that vent noxious odors out of the building.

Early forensic anthropologists had no access to such modern conveniences, and processed the bones wherever they could find a stove. Bill Bass once used his kitchen—with disastrous results for his wife's stove. He recalls, "They say: A watched pot never boils. However, an unattended one—at least if it's filled with human bones and decomposing flesh—swiftly bubbles over. I left my post at the stove just long enough to go to

Unearthed bones must be thoroughly cleaned in the lab before they can be properly studied.

the bathroom; when I returned, a froth of water, brain soup, and other foul-smelling components was pouring over the rim and seeping into every recess of Ann's stove. It would never be the same."[19]

When the maceration process is complete, the bones are scrubbed, rinsed, and laid out on a long table, face up, in anatomical order: The skull is placed at one end, followed by the shoulder and arm bones, ribs, pelvis, legs, and feet. Then the anthropologist can begin to determine several essential facts. As Bass and Jefferson note, "Before you can tell who someone was and how they died . . . you start with the Big Four: sex, race, age, and stature."[20]

Determining Height

Determining stature, or height, is relatively easy with a complete set of bones. All an anthropologist has to do is lay them out in anatomical order with tiny gaps between everything to account for cartilage that was originally present. The entire skeleton can then be measured.

Even if most of the skeleton is missing, the victim's height can still be determined. With only a single bone—usually one of the long leg or arm bones—anthropologists can determine height using an osteometric board, a sliding rectangular device that looks like a pair of bookends attached to a yardstick. The head of the board is fixed, but the foot is movable. The bone is placed with one end against the head of the board, and then the foot of the board is moved until it is pressed snugly against the other end of the bone.

The measurement shown on the board is plugged into a formula created by scientists who have studied the human body. These experts found that the proportions of the body—the length of the long leg bone as compared to the total height of a person, for instance—is almost always the same. Using this formula, bone experts are able to estimate a victim's height with only a small degree of error.

Teeth Will Tell

Determining a victim's age at death simply by looking at bones is more difficult than determining height. The skeleton changes in various ways as a person grows older, however, and bone experts look for such changes as they examine the remains.

When trying to establish age, anthropologists begin with the skull, if it is available. The teeth can provide invaluable information. If they are still deciduous "baby teeth," the victim was likely younger than five. If only the permanent incisors and first molars have erupted, the victim was about six or seven years old. If

By the Numbers

14%

Percentage of murders committed with knives or cutting instruments in the United States

the lateral incisors are present, the victim was seven or eight. If permanent canine teeth are present, the age is judged to be ten or eleven. If all the permanent teeth have erupted, the victim was at least seventeen years old. Worn or missing teeth can indicate the victim was middle-aged or older.

In addition to teeth, anthropologists look at cranial sutures—the zigzag seams between the bones of the skull. Bass and Jefferson explain, "Most people think of the cranium [that portion of the skull enclosing the brain] as a single dome of bone, and if you run your hands over the top of your head, it certainly feels like one piece. In reality, though, the cranial vault is a complex assembly of seven separate bones."[21]

In children, cranial sutures are separated by cartilage, which is replaced by bone as the child ages. Thus, experts know if the cranial sutures are apparent, the victim was relatively young. If some sutures are fused and others are not, the victim was between twenty and forty years old. If they are fully fused, the victim was middle-aged or older.

The Aging Body

The amount of cartilage in other bones in the body can also give indications of age. In children, the long bones are made up of a bony shaft and two bony end pieces held together with cartilage. With age, the cartilage is gradually replaced by bone. Most long bones are fully fused by the age of twenty-eight, so anthropologists can determine by the amount of cartilage remaining whether a victim was younger or older than that age.

If all the bones are fused, anthropologists look at other bones to help determine the age of the victim. They first examine the pubic symphysis—the joint at the front of the pelvis where the two pubic bones join. The inner surface of the pubic symphysis of a twenty-year-old is corrugated, or bumpy. By the thirties the bone has become smooth. By the age of forty or so, arthritis, osteoporosis, and the wear and tear caused by walking have worn its edges into sharp ridges, and its face has eroded to have a porous, spongy look.

Ribs also exhibit signs of age. In youth, for instance, the end of the fourth rib where it attaches to the sternum (breastbone) is rounded and smooth. As a person ages, the end of the rib becomes hollowed out or cup shaped, and the edges become increasingly jagged. Emily Craig notes, "The ends of our ribs are stressed every time we take a breath, while the bones of our pelvis grate together throughout our entire lives. The amount of movement is usually so minuscule that we don't even notice it—yet over time that movement is enough to wear down the underlying bone in ways that an anthropologist can use to read a person's age."[22]

In older victims, anthropologists can also turn to the microscope to determine age. Using a wafer-thin slice of bone, they can inspect the bone's osteons. With age, osteons tend to break, so by comparing the number of fragmented osteons to the number of healthy ones and applying those numbers to a mathematical formula, the victim's age can be estimated.

Two forensic scientists use teeth to help them determine the age of a victim of genocide.

Bones in the Human Body

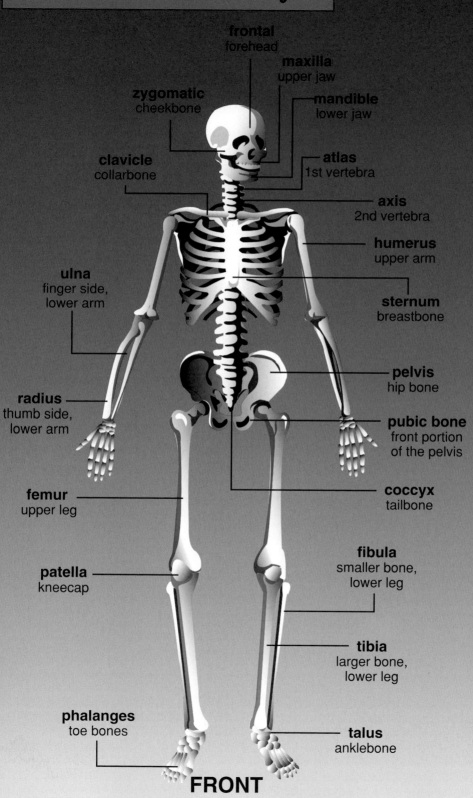

frontal
forehead

maxilla
upper jaw

zygomatic
cheekbone

mandible
lower jaw

clavicle
collarbone

atlas
1st vertebra

axis
2nd vertebra

humerus
upper arm

ulna
finger side,
lower arm

sternum
breastbone

radius
thumb side,
lower arm

pelvis
hip bone

pubic bone
front portion
of the pelvis

femur
upper leg

coccyx
tailbone

fibula
smaller bone,
lower leg

patella
kneecap

tibia
larger bone,
lower leg

phalanges
toe bones

talus
anklebone

FRONT

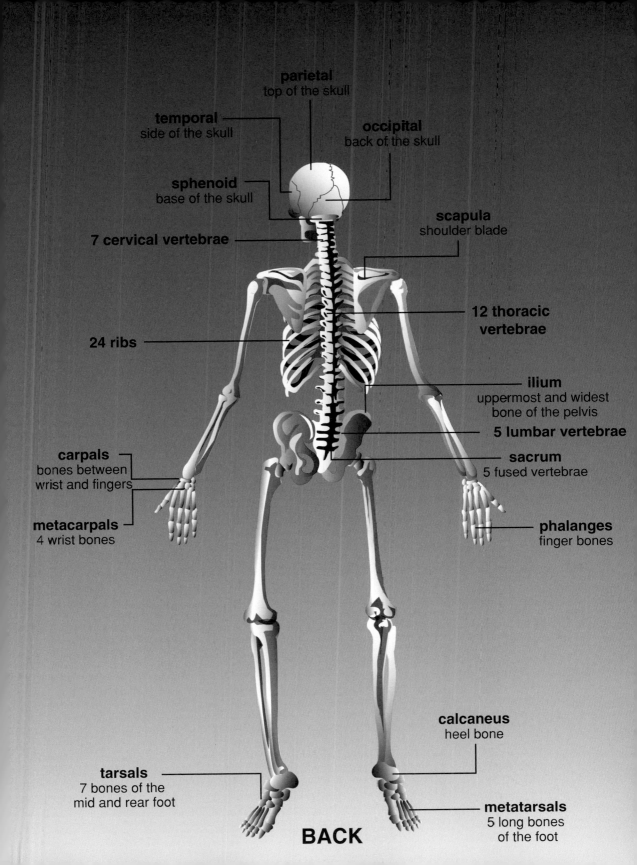

parietal
top of the skull

temporal
side of the skull

occipital
back of the skull

sphenoid
base of the skull

scapula
shoulder blade

7 cervical vertebrae

**12 thoracic
vertebrae**

24 ribs

ilium
uppermost and widest
bone of the pelvis

5 lumbar vertebrae

carpals
bones between
wrist and fingers

sacrum
5 fused vertebrae

metacarpals
4 wrist bones

phalanges
finger bones

calcaneus
heel bone

tarsals
7 bones of the
mid and rear foot

metatarsals
5 long bones
of the foot

BACK

Douglas Ubelaker remembers one Tennessee case in which he gauged the age of the victim using this method: "I called in my estimate of age [to the authorities in Tennessee] on a Friday afternoon; and as it happened, the body was identified that same day. The technique had permitted me to come within two years of the man's actual age at death; he had been nearly fifty-five."[23]

Determining Race

Determining the racial background of a victim is just as important as determining height or age. Although civil rights advocates object to racial distinctions because they are often linked to insinuations of inferiority, leading to discrimination and prejudice, forensic anthropologists rely on them because they help identify victims. Bass notes, "As the world's peoples increasingly mingle, traditional racial distinctions and labels may eventually blur and even disappear, but in the meantime I'll hang on to them, because they help me identify the dead and they help police solve murders."[24]

Anthropologists traditionally recognize three racial groups when it comes to bones, particularly skulls. Skulls of people of European ancestry are characterized by their elongated shape, recessive cheekbones, round eye sockets that are set close together, and long, narrow nasal openings.

People of African ancestry generally have skulls that are heavier and smoother than people of European ancestry. The eye sockets are rectangular, the nasal opening is broad, and the teeth and lower jaw jut forward in a trait called prognathism. Asian and Native American skulls are rounder than those of other racial groups. Flat cheekbones and nasal openings create the impression of a flat face. The eye sockets are round, and the front teeth can be distinctive because of ridges on their inside edges that make them shovel-shaped.

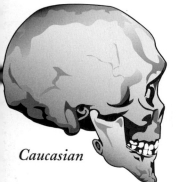

Caucasian

African

Asian

In the lab, a forensic anthropologist is able to determine that bones exhumed from a mass grave in Serbia belong to an ethnic Albanian.

Determining Gender

The lower jaw is curved in males but straight in females.

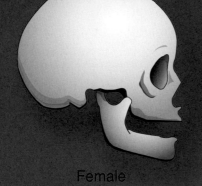

Female

Male

The female pelvis is wider than the male pelvis, and the sciatic notch is broader in females than in males.

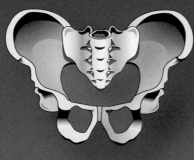

Female

Male

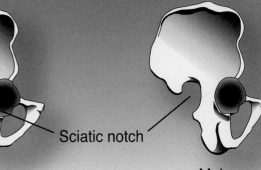

Sciatic notch

Female

Male

Sex-Marked Features

The gender of a skeleton is generally easier to determine than its age or race. Female bones are smoother and smaller than the bones of males, which tend to be heavy and have raised ridges where large muscles were once attached. A female skull is likely to have a more pointed chin, while a male chin will be square with a flared jaw line. A male skull will have heavy ridges above the eyebrows and a bony bump—the external occipital protuberance—at the back of the skull.

The pelvic bones are an extremely reliable indicator of gender. The female pelvis must allow a baby to pass through during childbirth. Thus the opening in the center—known as the pelvic inlet—is wide and shallow. The ilium (the hip bone that is felt on the side just below the waist) also has a notch along its edge that is wider than 50 degrees.

The bones of the male pelvis are generally heavier than those of the female pelvis, and the pelvic opening is narrow, deep, and heart shaped. The notch on the ilium is less than 50 degrees. Forensic anthropologists know that if a thumb placed in the notch has room to wiggle, the victim was female. If the thumb fits tightly in the notch, the victim was male.

Determining the sex of a child's skeleton is extremely difficult even for the best anthropologists. This is because before the sex glands become functional, the hormonal changes that cause the female pelvis to broaden and make male bones and muscles grow heavier have not yet occurred. Craig observes, "I can usually tell the sex of an adult arm or leg bone by measuring its size at the joint or by finding sex-marked features in a pelvis or in some . . . feature such as muscle insertions. . . . With young children, it's harder, since boys' and girls' bones pretty much resemble each other until puberty."[25]

Other Stories in the Bones

Anthropologists can get other information from bones in addition to height, age, race, and sex. Sometimes the unique features they detect can help match a name to a set of remains and even lead to the solution of a crime.

Handedness is one such feature. After a lifetime of use, a person's bones reflect which arm was used most often for activities that range from writing to hammering nails or swinging a tennis racket. This use causes the muscles of the dominant arm and hand to develop more than those in the other arm, and the ridges where those muscles attach to the bones become knobbier and rougher than those on the other arm. The socket in the scapula (shoulder blade) of the dominant arm will also be more worn and grooved from the ball of the humerus (the long bone of the upper arm) moving in it. Thus, if a missing person is known to be left-handed, and a set of remains shows that the left arm was the dominant arm, the possibility of a match exists. Because there are many left-handed people in the world, however, other factors must also match before a positive identification can be made.

Injury and Illness

Changes in bone due to occupation or injury are easily detected and can be good indicators that lead to identification of a victim. If a missing person was known to have played a clarinet or an oboe professionally, for instance, and the remains exhibit distinctive large knobs on the hinge of the jaw where the cheek muscles continually pulled, the examiner would consider a match highly likely. If a missing person was a professional athlete known to have had knee injuries, and the remains show signs of scar tissue and healed bones in that area, that too would be considered a likely match.

Certain diseases and illnesses also leave clear marks for anthropologists to read. If a victim suffered from osteomyelitis, an infection that causes destruction of the bone and new bone formation, that could be detected during an inspection of the remains. X-ray examination of the remains of a person who suffered arrested growth as a result of poor diet or a long illness would reveal a series of transverse white lines known as

How DNA Is Obtained from Bones

DNA analysis of bone is difficult and costly, but when all else fails, anthropologists turn to this procedure to help make an identification. To obtain the genetic material, they take the following steps:

1 **A bone sample** is sterilized and dried.

2 **Using a drill**, a small amount of powdered bone is obtained.

3 **Bone powder is placed** in a test tube and mixed with a special extracting solution.

4 **The solution is heated**, then centrifuged (spun in a centrifuge machine) so that the portion containing DNA is released from the bone tissue and rises to the top.

5 **The DNA solution** is collected, mixed with chloroform/isoamyl alcohol, and again centrifuged.

6 **The upper solution** containing the DNA is collected.

7 **The DNA solution is mixed** with purifying solution and centrifuged. This step is repeated two to three times until the DNA is pure.

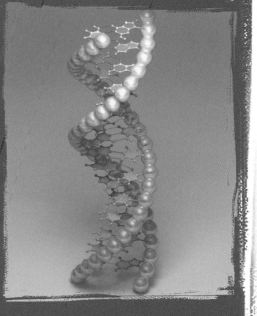

This model depicts the double-helix structure of DNA, which can be extracted from bones to identify human remains.

This forensic scientist will extract DNA from a tooth to help identify the remains of a victim of the 2004 Indian Ocean tsunami.

lines of arrested growth. Measurement of these lines could even provide information as to when the retardation of growth took place and, in the case of a child, could be used to prove that the victim had suffered from long-term neglect.

DNA from Bones

When visual or microscopic examination of the bones does not lead to identification, anthropologists turn to DNA analysis to help identify the victim. The processes of extracting and replicating DNA can be long and expensive, however, and even if a DNA profile is obtained, there may be no way to match the remains with an identity. Craig says, "Most people's genetic material is not on file. . . . For the process to work . . . you need two kinds of reports on file: missing persons and unidentified remains."[26]

Although DNA from the nucleus of cells is extremely fragile and difficult to come by when working with bones, mitochondrial DNA (mtDNA), located outside the nucleus of the cell in organelles known as mitochondria, is more durable and stable. There is usually enough usable mtDNA in bone cells to create a profile even if the bones or teeth are very old or degraded. If not, a technique called polymerase chain reaction, in which a small amount of DNA is chemically copied, can be used to produce enough to create a profile. Because mtDNA is passed unchanged from mother to child, if the identity of a victim is suspected, the profile can be compared to that of a sibling, the mother, or a close relative on the mother's side.

DNA might identify a victim, but it never tells the story of how the victim died. For that vital information, anthropologists again turn to a visual examination of the bones. As William Maples noted, "They [speak] secrets to me and to my students, yielding up hidden information, furnishing ideas and evidence to the world of the living. . . . Remains such as these have established innocence or guilt. They have pointed the way to the electric chair."[27]

CHAPTER 3

Broken Bones

Determining the cause of death from skeletal remains can seem like an impossible task for those who are not familiar with bones. Bone experts know, however, that even the tiniest fragments can reveal the most vital evidence of all—evidence indicating whether foul play took place, and if so, what instrument was used to carry out the murder. Maples recalled:

> I have seen the tiny, wisp-thin bones of a murdered infant stand up in court and crush a bold, hardened, adult killer, sending him pale and penitent to the electric chair. A small fragment of a woman's skullcap, gnawed by alligators and found by accident at the bottom of a river, furnished enough evidence for me to help convict a hatchet murderer, two years after the fact.[28]

Green Bones

Determining cause of death involves recognizing the distinctive marks left by all kinds of weapons on bones. It also requires the ability to judge when the wounds were inflicted—a significant time before death (antemortem), around the time of death (perimortem), or after death (postmortem). To make such judgments, forensic anthropologists must first be familiar with the differences between living bone and old bone.

Living bone is also known as green bone because it resembles green, living wood. It is alive, fluid filled, and always growing and changing. It can bend and twist without breaking. It also has a slightly greasy feeling and a distinct odor. Dead bone, on the other hand, resembles old wood. It lacks

A team of forensic anthropologists studies skeletal remains of victims of Guatemala's civil war in order to determine the precise causes of death.

moisture and becomes increasingly dry and brittle as time passes. When bent or twisted, it is likely to snap rather than bend. If left to freeze, it develops lacy cracks on its surface.

When it comes to color, green bone is a creamy yellow, while old bone is often almost white from exposure to sun and rain. Because old bone is more porous, however, it can also take on the color of the environment around it. For instance, an old bone lying on soil that is very dark because it contains organic material like rotten wood and leaves will turn dark brown. So if anthropologists find a very light skull half-buried in dark organic soil, they would suggest that it had been deposited there fairly recently because it had not yet taken on the color of the earth around it.

Murder or Something Else?

Forensic anthropologists know bone so well that they are well qualified to judge not only how the natural environment affects it, but also how and when man-made marks were inflicted. An antemortem mark will be healed. Scar tissue will have formed over nicks caused by bullets or cut marks caused by sharp objects. Breaks will have grown back together. Such will not be the case with new trauma. Ubelaker describes a case in which he detected both antemortem and perimortem injuries on a victim's skull: "The earlier trauma was to the victim's nose, evidenced by remodeling of the bone, possibly the result of an old fight. At about the time of death the nose was again broken in the same place, and the new fracture line intersected or paralleled the healed tissue from the earlier incident."[29]

Damage that occurs to bones long after death is easier to identify than wounds that occurred around the time of death. Signs of chipping or shattering usually indicate that the bone was dead and brittle when trauma occurred. If the bone is still fairly fresh, however, damage will look much the same whether it was caused by a murderer or by careless handling during and after recovery. Ubelaker notes, "I have had numerous cases in which I identified clearly defined cut marks on bone, only to

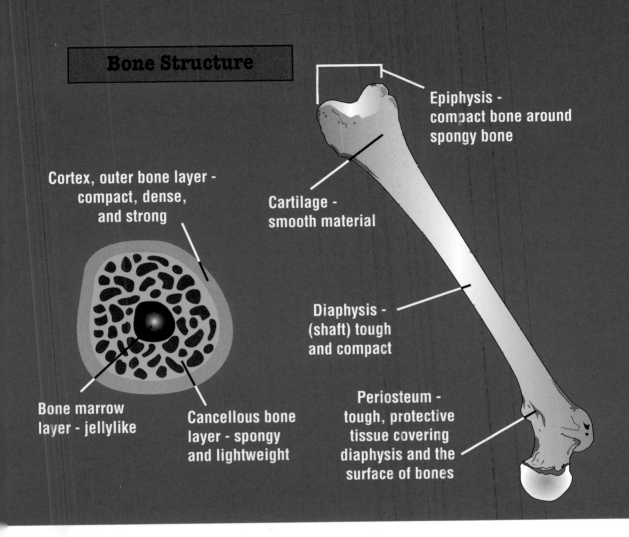

Bone Structure

Epiphysis - compact bone around spongy bone

Cortex, outer bone layer - compact, dense, and strong

Cartilage - smooth material

Diaphysis - (shaft) tough and compact

Bone marrow layer - jellylike

Cancellous bone layer - spongy and lightweight

Periosteum - tough, protective tissue covering diaphysis and the surface of bones

find after reporting them that the local examiner had used a scalpel or strong knife to cut away the soft tissue, leaving a whole series of little nicks which were indistinguishable from the evidence of assault."[30]

Damage to bone caused by animals during the postmortem period can also confuse inexperienced examiners. Ubelaker observes, "I have seen numerous examples of carnivore damage mistakenly associated with cause of death, and I have also seen cases in which the real cause of death was hidden among the tooth marks of a rat or dog."[31] The best forensic anthropologists easily recognize the kinds of marks animals leave on bones, however. They know that dogs, wolves, and coyotes leave irregular scrape marks as they chew at the end of a leg or arm

Truth in the Bones

When serial killer Jeffrey Dahmer confessed that his first murder took place in 1978 in his hometown of Bath, Ohio, police went searching for evidence to support his claim. Dahmer said he had killed an eighteen-year-old hitchhiker named Steven Hicks, dismembered his body, crushed the remains with a sledgehammer, and scattered them in the woods near his home. The area was thoroughly searched in 1991, yielding a variety of artifacts that included animal as well as human bones. Of the latter, some were less than ½ inch (1.27 cm) long. The largest was just over 2 inches (5.08cm).

Authorities sent the bones to Douglas Owsley, an anthropologist at the Smithsonian Institution. Owsley and his assistant sorted out the various animal bones, then painstakingly

Serial killer Jeffrey Dahmer dismembered and mutilated the body of his first victim.

examined the human remains. Some of the fragments bore cut marks, supporting Dahmer's statement that he had dismembered Hicks. When the fragments were pieced together, they were found to be of a male consistent with Hicks's height and age. Finally, Owsley obtained medical and dental X-rays taken of Hicks before he disappeared and compared them to fragments of teeth and vertebrae that had been recovered. The match was exact, and authorities announced that a positive identification of Hicks had been made.

bone. Bears leave puncture marks as their canine teeth clamp down on the centers of long bones. Rats and mice chew along the edges of bones, leaving vertical scrapes that correspond to their sharp, pointed teeth.

Sharp-Force Trauma

After forensic anthropologists eliminate ante- and postmortem trauma, they are left with damage that took place at or very near to the time of death. This can include the injury that actually killed the victim as well as accompanying trauma ranging from broken ribs to incineration. Injuries are judged to have occurred during the perimortem period if they are associated with the cause of death, and if the bone responded like living bone.

When analyzing perimortem trauma, examiners divide injuries into four categories: those caused by sharp force, blunt force, gunshot, and fire. Sharp-force trauma involves impressions left by sharp objects—knives, axes, scissors, and so forth.

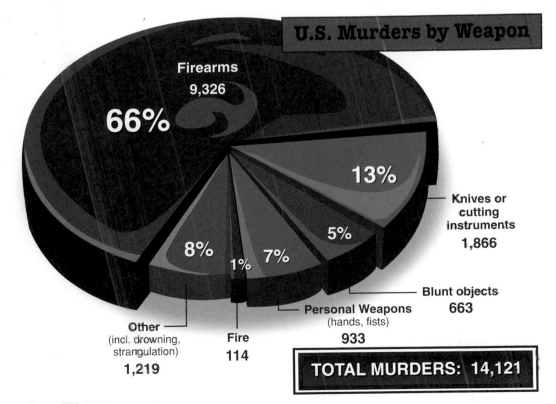

U.S. Murders by Weapon

Firearms
9,326
66%

13%
Knives or cutting instruments
1,866

5%

8% **1%** **7%**

Blunt objects
663

Personal Weapons
(hands, fists)
933

Other
(incl. drowning, strangulation)
1,219

Fire
114

TOTAL MURDERS: 14,121

Source: FBI, 2004.

By the Numbers

663
Number of victims murdered by blunt instruments in the United States in 2004

If they hit bone, these weapons leave an assortment of marks such as nicks, punctures, slice marks, or V- or U-shaped grooves.

The characteristic reaction of living bone to sharp force is called the green bone response: The cut edge of the bone raises and curls in a distinctive way along the edges. If a large piece of bone is sliced loose with a knife, for instance, it is likely to curve up and outward. If a small nick is made, the edges will curl slightly inward in a way that is easily apparent to a skilled examiner. Emily Craig notes, "Cut marks made at or around the time of death look completely different from those made [long] after death—if you know what to look for."[32]

When anthropologists look at a skeleton for evidence of sharp-force trauma, they often examine the ribs first. This is because many attackers stab their victims in the chest or back, and the blade bounces off a rib before plunging deeper. By laying out the bones in anatomical order, examiners are often able to interpret the nicks and gouges to determine the angle at which the blows were delivered.

Examiners also look for evidence of nicks or cuts on the bones of the forearms and hands. These marks, known as defense wounds, are the result of victims raising their hands and arms to protect themselves during an attack. Defense wounds are always classed as perimortem trauma, because the victim was alive and fending off an attack when they occurred.

Saws and Dismemberment

Saws, which come into play when a killer cuts apart a victim, cause a unique kind of sharp-force trauma. In the mid-1900s, hacksaws were the weapons of choice for dismemberments because they were readily available and easy to dispose of, and their fine, serrated blades quickly cut through bone. According to Maples, "It is a lot easier to saw through a human bone with a hacksaw than with a wood saw. I have verified this myself."[33]

In recent years, many killers turned to chainsaws to dismember their victims. Chainsaws are faster and require less effort, but they are also louder and throw blood and tissue in all directions. Like all saws, they leave distinctive cuts. Maples and Browning observe, "There is no way to cut a body up and leave no traces of the tools you use. Hew [cut] at them though you may, bones yet will have their say."[34]

Saw mark experts have learned by careful study the various patterns that different saws make on bone as they pass through it. Craig writes, "A chainsaw rips and chews through the bone in an instant, leaving gouges and chips in its wake, while a serrated knife leaves a pattern of dips and points—not to be confused with the straight, smooth cut mark often left by a butcher knife or a meat cleaver."[35] Experts can see differences between push marks and pull marks left when a killer wields a hand saw. They can tell when the killer hesitated, or made a false start, moved the saw, and started again. They know that hacksaw blades leave fine, straight marks that overlap. They can tell one chainsaw model from another by the pattern the chain leaves as its passes across thick bone surfaces.

As a result of their skills, saw experts can use something as simple as the width of the saw blade to help convict a killer. During his examination of skeletal remains in a murder case in the early 1990s, forensic anthropologist Steven A. Symes noted that the victim, Leslie Mahaffy, had been dismembered with a circular saw that had a blade much thinner than the usual carbon-tipped ones, which leave a groove of

In recent years, some killers have used chainsaws to dismember their victims.

about ¹⁄₈ inch (.32cm) wide. The saw retrieved from a lake where accused murderer Paul Bernardo had disposed of it had a blade that was indeed thinner and finer-toothed than modern carbon-tipped blades. Bass and Jefferson observe, "The blade . . . fit Steve's cut-mark analysis to a T."[36] Symes testified in court and Bernardo was found guilty.

Blunt-Force Trauma

While saws leave distinct impressions, blunt-force trauma is more difficult to identify. Blunt-force trauma is injury that results from a blow or blows from instruments such as hammers, rocks, baseball bats, or even hands or feet. Experts know, however, that when they see a skull that is cracked or a long bone that is not completely broken (known as a greenstick fracture), they are often looking at damage caused by blunt force.

A broken hyoid bone, the small horseshoe-shaped bone located in the neck just beneath the base of the tongue, is a sure sign of blunt force trauma. When a victim is strangled, the hyoid is often damaged. When a child is the victim, however, fracture may not occur because the bones are more flexible.

Sometimes a blunt instrument actually leaves an identifying mark on the bones. For instance, the shaft of a golf club can leave a long, narrow groove. The round end of a ball-peen hammer can leave a ball-shaped indentation. In a May 1990 case, mill worker Melvin Lloyd White killed one of his friends by hitting him over the head with a tire iron after a party. When Ubelaker examined the skull, the crescent-shaped impression

Blunt-force trauma injuries, such as those caused by a sledgehammer, are extremely difficult to identify.

Expert Witnesses

Forensic anthropologists often serve as expert witnesses when cases on which they have worked come to trial. Whether they represent the defense or the prosecution, they are ethically responsible for presenting the facts as clearly, accurately, and objectively as possible.

Like all expert witnesses, forensic anthropologists are allowed to give their scientific opinion in a trial if it relates to their area of expertise. They must first convince the judge that they are qualified in their field. Then, being careful not to make unwarranted assumptions, they state what they believe the facts mean. For instance, instead of saying that a victim was shot in the head, a forensic anthropologist is likely to state, "I saw a circular defect in the skull that demonstrates internal beveling. Internal beveling is a characteristic of entrance gunshot wounds."

Evidence collected from mass graves discovered in Iraq by forensic anthropologist Joan Bytheway was used against Saddam Hussein during his trial.

of the iron was clear and exactly fit the weapon. Ubelaker remembers testifying at White's trial: "When I finally did get to testify before the jury, I stood before them with the skull in one hand and the iron bar in the other and demonstrated how the lug wrench [end] fitted exactly inside the punch hole. It was damning evidence."[37]

Gunshot Trauma

Trauma caused by a bullet can be mistaken for blunt-force trauma because when the projectile strikes a bone, the bone often breaks. The bullet can merely perforate the bone, leaving a punched-out hole, or it can slide along it, leaving pulverized bone behind.

When a bullet pierces a piece of flat green bone, such as a skull, the hole it makes is small and round, with a beveled (sloped or angled) inside edge. Beveling occurs when the inner layer of bone around the edge of the hole breaks away, leaving the outer layer around the hole intact. When a bullet exits through bone, the hole is larger and somewhat jagged because the bullet pushes bone fragments and soft tissue in front of it as it passes through the body. An exit hole is beveled on the outside.

Even trained bone experts can have difficulty determining whether an irregular mark on bone is gunshot trauma, so X-rays are often taken of the area to see if lead particles were left by the bullet's passing. In the case of Glyde Earl Meek, who killed his girlfriend and set his cabin on fire before committing suicide by a shot to the head, X-rays revealed molten buckshot fused to the inner lining of his skull and traces of lead on the lower jaw. Maples observed, "Clearly a shotgun barrel had been inserted into the

Because gunshot trauma can sometimes be mistaken for blunt-force trauma, X-rays are often taken of the injury to reveal traces of lead.

mouth . . . and the weapon had been fired before the fire consumed both his body and the wooden parts of the gun that killed him."[38]

Trauma by Fire

As in the Meek case, murderers often use fire to try to erase the evidence of their crimes. Fire can be devastating to bones. It causes skulls to split apart and burns up small pieces completely. As they carbonize, even large bones blacken, then become gray, then white as all of the organic material burns away, leaving only mineral components. Such bones are called calcined bones and are extremely fragile, often crumbling at the slightest touch.

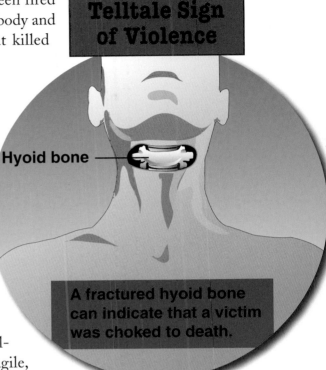

Telltale Sign of Violence

Hyoid bone

A fractured hyoid bone can indicate that a victim was choked to death.

Anthropologists know that no matter how hot a fire is, however, there are likely to be remains left afterward. Craig writes, "Trying to burn a human body—which after all is about 80 percent water—is like trying to burn a huge, sopping sponge. The fluid-filled organs, muscles, and bones can often withstand the fiercest of flames."[39] Bone experts can get a great deal of information from those remains. For instance, if the skeleton is lying in a "pugilistic" or "boxer" position— posed as if to fight with the legs bent, the arms pulled up to the chest, and the hands balled into fists—investigators know the bones were covered with flesh when the fire started and that they were twisted and warped by fluids, fat, and the pull of the muscles as they burned.

Anthropologists can also read burned bones to find evidence of injuries that may indicate murder. To do this, they often have to put burned fragments back together again as if they were puzzle pieces, matching them according to thickness, curvature, and other distinguishing characteristics. Maples wrote, "I cannot hope to convey the immense, fatiguing and yet fascinating task of reassembling . . . fragments. We used Duco cement—model airplane glue—to put the bones back together because it does not expand when subjected to moisture, and because you can always dissolve it with acetone if you make a mistake."[40]

When the bones are reassembled, trauma can be plain to see. In the investigation that followed the 1993 burning of the Branch Davidian compound in Waco, Texas, forensic anthropologists found signs of bullet holes in the rebuilt skulls of many of the eighty members who died there. The most significant find was a hole in the center of the forehead of leader David Koresh's skull. The hole was ringed with soot, showing that the shot had been fired at close range, evidence of suicide or murder by a close associate.

Sometimes burned fragments are scarce or cannot be reassembled. Still, bone experts can often get enough information from them to help solve a crime. In one 1997 case, a Kentucky couple named Gary and Sophie Stephens seemed to have vanished until fragments of burned bone were found behind the toolbox in their abandoned pickup truck. Further investigation led to a bonfire site, where ashes and tiny shards of bone were recovered.

After carefully sifting the ashes, Craig retrieved a surgical fixation staple that was the same make, model, and size of one that had been used to repair Gary's injured knee a few years earlier. Craig also found a porcelain crown that matched Sophie's dental records and a fragment of vertebra with a pellet of birdshot embedded in it. The last proved that at least one of the Stephenses had been shot in the back. The Stephenses' son, Gary, eventually confessed to the mur-

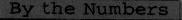

By the Numbers

114

Number of victims murdered in fires in the United States in 2004

ders and was sentenced to life in prison. Craig later recalled, "The . . . case taught me a valuable lesson—no detail is too small to be useful, especially when you're dealing with victims who have been destroyed by fire."[41]

Identifying one or two victims using shards of bone is challenging for even the best forensic anthropologists. The difficulties are magnified many times in the case of mass murder, when the bones of uncounted victims—sometimes charred by fire, sometimes mixed helter-skelter in a mass grave—need to be sorted and then matched with names. Despite the obstacles, however, bone experts are willing to take on such daunting tasks because it is a part of their compelling calling. Craig says, "Whether you're dealing with one victim or several hundred, the rules remain the same: Go slow, keep an eye out for details—and always be prepared to be surprised."[42]

Forensic anthropologists must sometimes work with nearly unrecognizable human remains, such as these unearthed in Bosnia.

CHAPTER 4

Sorting the Bones

Cases that involve mass murder are some of the most demanding for forensic anthropologists. Called in by governments, victims' families, and human rights groups, they travel to countries like Chile, Argentina, Bosnia, and Rwanda to help investigate deaths carried out by abusive governments. They also help identify victims of serial killings and mass disasters such as those that occurred in Waco, Texas, in 1993; Oklahoma City in 1995; and New York City in 2001.

The work is frustrating, exhausting, and time consuming. At the same time, it is extremely rewarding because it gives closure to hundreds of families who would otherwise never know what happened to their loved ones. It also allows government leaders to be called to account for crimes they might otherwise get away with. Clyde Snow, who has led many overseas teams, states, "The great mass murderers of our time have accounted for no more than a few hundred victims. In contrast, states that have chosen to murder their own citizens can usually count their victims by the carload lot."[43]

The Disappeared

Snow's first experience identifying victims of human rights abuse was in Argentina in 1984. He and a team of volunteers were asked by the National Commission on the Disappeared, an Argentine human rights group, to exhume, identify, and establish cause of death for the more than twenty thousand victims of the former military government's so-called Dirty War between 1976 and 1983. Government leaders were alleged to have kidnapped, tortured, and killed those they considered enemies, including trade union members, students, and anyone holding opposing political views.

Cases involving mass murder are particularly challenging for forensic anthropologists. These scientists are collecting evidence from a mass grave in Bosnia.

Working a Mass Grave

Forensic anthropologists draw on their archeology experience when working a mass grave. They proceed as follows:

1. **The size of the grave,** soil density, and hardness is determined using probes.

2. **The site is cordoned off** to establish its boundaries and prevent passersby from entering.

3. **Backhoes or workers with shovels** remove shallow layers of dirt until the first sign of bodies or other evidence appears.

4. **Excavators,** dressed in overalls, boots, and gloves to protect themselves from contamination, enter the site with trowels and brushes.

5. **The site is divided** into sections, which are worked individually.

6. **Dirt is gently brushed away** from bones and other evidence until they are completely exposed.

7. **Photographs are taken** of each bone and piece of evidence.

8. **Bones are mapped** on the site.

9. **Each piece of evidence** is placed in a bag and marked for identification purposes.

10. **Each set of bones** is bagged, labeled, and sent to the lab for further examination.

Snow and his team went to Argentina with little idea of how long the project would take. They found that bulldozers and men with spades had excavated some of the suspected graves and heaped all the bones they found in piles. In other situations, exhumed bones had been thrown into bags and awaited examination in morgues. Medical and dental records that might have been used to establish identity had been lost or were incomplete.

Nevertheless, the team began their work with the care and thoughtfulness characteristic of anthropologists in the field. In cemeteries where some of the victims were believed to have been buried, test probes were dug to determine the depth of burial. The surface soil was then removed with picks and shovels. When the first body was reached, diggers scraped away the dirt with trowels and spoons until the bones were completely unearthed. At one of the graves, the first find was a skull. "There was a bullet hole right up over the eye," Snow says, noting that beveling proved the victim had been shot at the time of death. "According to my experience, it [looked] like an execution-style wound."[44]

Forensic Anthropology Teams

As the work progressed, the team made identifications and observed further signs of violence. In April 1985 Snow left the field to testify at the trial of the nine generals and admirals who had helped govern Argentina during the Dirty War. The photos he presented of bones pocked by shotgun pellets consistent with guns used by the Argentine army and police in the 1970s proved compelling. So did his explanation of what the wounds meant—that the deceased had been shot at close range in a vital spot such as the head, chest, or back. "In many ways the skeleton is its own best witness,"[45] he stated as he concluded testimony that helped convict five of the nine.

> **By the Numbers**
>
> # 90%
>
> **Percentage of murders committed by males in the United States.**

Snow's work in Argentina was important not only because it helped to bring killers to justice, but also because it helped give rise to the independent, nonprofit Argentine Forensic Anthropology Team (Equipo Argentino de Antropología Forense, or EAAF) in 1984. The EAAF was founded to investigate and document human rights violations worldwide using forensic science, particularly forensic anthropology and archaeology. Members assist relatives of victims in their efforts to recover remains, testify in court regarding their findings in the field, and lead seminars on the application of forensic science for humanitarian purposes. They also work to reveal the truth of history in countries where governments try to distort or hide it.

Other groups soon joined the EAAF as it conducted exhumations and investigations in countries ranging from Guatemala to East Timor. Mercedes Doretti, an original member of the Argentine team, observes, "Our work helps in the historic reconstruction that is often hidden by the authorities and the governments that took part in [the violations]. Even though we talk about bones, they represent faces and histories."[46]

War Crimes

In the 1990s Bosnia-Herzegovina was the site of some of the most far-reaching forensic excavations anthropologists had ever performed in their efforts to prove human rights abuses. A civil war had been fought in the region between 1992 and 1995, and reports of mass executions in Srebrenica, Bosnia, and Vukovar, Croatia, led to a global demand for an investigation. Because of the massive amount of work to be done, the EAAF, Physicians for Human Rights, and forensic scientists from nineteen countries were called in to assist.

As they had in previous investigations, teams proceeded slowly and methodically so as not to destroy vital evidence. Positioning of bodies could provide clues about how the killings had been carried out, so it was important to dig carefully. Once remains were uncovered, each set was photographed and its exact location was mapped with an electronic surveying system.

The work seemed never ending at times, and was always sobering. Nevertheless, the teams remained motivated and focused, because they knew what was as stake. "You never get used to it—never," says anthropologist Fredy Peccerelli, who worked with Snow in Guatemala and was president of the Guatemala Forensic Anthropology Foundation. "It's still somebody who died who shouldn't have been killed."[47]

Serial Victims

In addition to uncovering human rights abuses around the world, forensic anthropologists use their skills in serial killing cases, especially when multiple sets of remains are found in one place. One of the most chilling of these investigations involved the home of killer John Wayne Gacy in Des Plaines, Illinois. When police became suspicious of Gacy and entered the crawl space under his house in December 1978, they found a mound that proved to be human remains.

Recovering them was not the end of the matter, however. Within days, careful excavation yielded twenty-seven bodies in various stages of decay. (Gacy was later charged with thirty-two murders.) Medical examiner Robert Stein, who helped process the site, said, "It's a maze down there. A maze. But the things in the maze are not marbles or checkers. They are bodies, the bodies of young men."[48] While most were found in the crawl space,

This skull, belonging to a genocide victim, was excavated from a mass grave in Serbia.

others came from under the garage and patio. The medical examiner's office did what it could to identify the unrecognizable victims. This included using information found in Gacy's home, as well as photos, X-rays, and dental records provided by families who suspected their loved ones might have been among the victims. After six weeks, however, more than half the victims remained nameless.

At that point the medical examiner called in Snow. Snow examined each set of remains for unique features that could lead to identification and painstakingly compared them with the remaining missing persons reports at his disposal. Authors Christopher Joyce and Eric Stover explain, "The final identifications . . . were the hardest; it was like picking up a cross-

Dr. Clyde Snow works painstakingly to assemble the skull of a victim of civil war in El Salvador.

word puzzle someone has abandoned and trying to fill in those last few spaces."[49]

In the end, Snow was able to successfully identify five victims. As Joyce and Stover point out, "For the five families whose sons Snow . . . had identified, a mystery had been solved, albeit with a sad ending."[50]

Mass Disaster

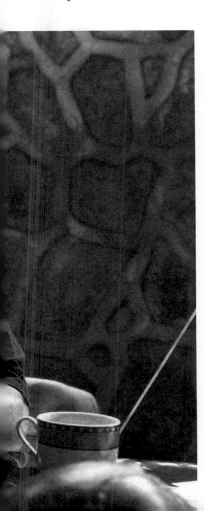

Snow is not the only bone expert with the skills to sort and identify the jumble of bones that remains after a mass tragedy. Beginning in the 1990s, forensic anthropologists, including Emily Craig, Harrell Gill-King, and Mary Manhein, became part of Disaster Mortuary Operational Response Teams (DMORT), groups of individuals who volunteer to identify victims and provide mortuary services after large-scale disasters. Now part of the U.S. Department of Homeland Security, ten regional DMORT divisions exist across the United States. Teams are composed of funeral directors, medical examiners, pathologists, forensic anthropologists, fingerprint specialists, forensic dentists, X-ray technicians, mental health specialists, computer professionals, administrative support staff, security and investigative personnel, and others. Craig writes, "Being in DMORT is a bit like being in the National Guard. . . . We keep our regular jobs, but when the country needs us to serve somewhere, we work things out with our bosses and go."[51]

As a crucial part of DMORT teams, anthropologists have responded

Responding to a Need

The roots of Disaster Mortuary Operational Response Teams (DMORT) can be traced to October 1990, when eighty-seven people lost their lives during a fire at the Happy Land Social Club in New York City. The incident was the second significant tragedy in the area in a period of two months, and the medical examiner's office was overwhelmed. The medical examiner thus turned to a group of funeral directors and asked them to assist the families of the victims. Under the leadership of Thomas J. Shepardson, a volunteer with the federal government's Office of Emergency Preparedness, the funeral directors set up a location for families to meet, get reports of their loved ones, and provide information that might help identify the victims.

Shepardson and his team soon recognized that they were filling a need that arose with every mass disaster. They went on to develop a plan wherein teams of doctors, morticians, police, counselors, and other personnel would be activated by government request, travel to a disaster site, and help local authorities. The result was DMORT, which over the next ten years grew into an organization of twelve hundred members.

Victims of the 1990 Happy Land Social Club fire lie covered by sheets before being examined by forensic specialists.

to disasters that range from the Oklahoma City bombing in 1995 to the New Orleans floods in 2005. One of the first mass disasters at which Craig worked was that of the siege of the Branch Davidian compound in 1993. Because it was unclear whether the fire—and the subsequent deaths of over eighty people—had been caused by the Branch Davidians or by law enforcement officials, the investigation was a criminal one. Craig and the two other anthropologists who helped examine the remains were aware that each piece of bone or tissue had to be treated as potential evidence, with every detail documented. Thus, the procedure they followed was always the same: Photographs were taken first; X-rays and analysis followed. A recorder stood by to take notes of everything that was found.

Craig's task was to try to identify the children who had perished in the compound. Most had not burned, but had suffocated in the smoke. Their bodies had decomposed before they were recovered, leaving only hair and bones.

Forensic anthropologist Dr. Emily Craig helped to identify victims of the fire at the Branch Davidian compound in 1993.

Craig used hair color and length to help with the identification. At other times, she rebuilt the tiny skulls and matched teeth and other features to any photographs of the children that were available. She remembers, "The children were the hardest to deal with—both scientifically and emotionally. . . . No matter how skilled or professional I might become, my elation at solving forensic problems would forever coexist with suppressed despair for the victims."[52]

Mass Homicide

Matching identities to remains was just as heart-wrenching but not as difficult for anthropologists who processed remains after the Oklahoma City bombing, when domestic terrorist

Timothy McVeigh blew up the Alfred P. Murrah Federal Building in 1995, killing 168 people and injuring hundreds more. McVeigh was angry about the federal government's treatment of Koresh and the Branch Davidians in 1993.

The Oklahoma City bombing was considered a mass homicide from the beginning, so officials wanted to recover and document every piece of evidence in order to prosecute whomever was responsible. Because of the unsafe condition of the building after the bombing, bodies were recovered from the rubble by search-and-rescue personnel, placed in body bags, and then taken to a temporary morgue where forensic specialists examined them.

Many of the bodies still had identifying characteristics when they were recovered, so fingerprints, teeth, clothing, and personal items could be matched with records provided by families, dentists, and doctors in the area. Many of those who died in the explosion worked in the building, so the identities of those missing were suspected from the beginning.

The Odd Leg

There were, however, instances in which body parts could not be easily identified, and then the skills of the anthropologists were invaluable. Craig was consulted after McVeigh's defense attorney claimed that a severed leg found close to the center of the blast belonged to "the real bomber." The defense postulated that this supposed bomber had been killed in the blast, and the leg was all that remained of him.

The leg was medium sized, sturdy, and shod in an army boot, but it was badly mutilated. FBI investigators were unable to say for certain whether it was male or female, black or Caucasian. Craig studied the limb for several hours, paying particular attention to the shape of the intercondylar notch,

By the Numbers

70%

Percentage of murders committed with firearms in the United States

the place where the thighbone fits into the knee joint. She knew from experience that the angle of the notch differs markedly according to ethnicity, and here the evidence was clear. She recalls, "By the end of the afternoon, I was ready to go on the record. . . . This leg had belonged to a woman—a woman who was undoubtedly Black."[53]

Craig was criticized by other experts for her determination, but she was proven right in February 1996 when the leg was matched to a twenty-one-year-old member of the US Air Force, Lakesha Levy—a black woman. An exhumation and examination proved Levy had been buried with someone else's left leg. Craig explains, "Mass fatality incidents usually involve

Forensic evidence collected from the site of the 1995 Oklahoma City bombing helped to convict Timothy McVeigh of the crime.

. . . commingling of bodies and body parts. . . . In this case, an unattached or 'unassociated' left leg from someone else had mistakenly been linked to Lakesha at the crime scene, an error that had somehow slipped by at autopsy."[54]

Twin Towers

The devastation caused by the Oklahoma City bombing paled in comparison to that experienced at the World Trade Center in lower Manhattan on September 11, 2001. The site was by far the largest crime scene forensic experts had ever seen. The tragedy marked the first time all ten DMORT teams from across the United States were activated. At the peak of the effort, almost three hundred team members lent their services to local workers in New York City.

Estimates were that more than 3,000 people lay dead among the tons of debris that had once been the World Trade Center. (The final number of confirmed dead was 2,748.) As bodies were recovered, few were found in one piece, and bone experts were in high demand to examine severely burned and damaged remains to identify what parts of the body they might have come from, and to determine the sex, age, stature, and so forth of the victims.

Some anthropologists arrived in Manhattan while the fires were still burning at Ground Zero. They immediately took their places in the temporary morgue that had been set up outside the city's permanent morgue to accommodate the many examination tables that were necessary. The noisy, overcrowded workplace was a far cry from the environments in which they usually worked. Anthropologist Anthony Falsetti, director of the C.A. Pound Identification Laboratory, began work three days after the attacks. He remarks, "Working at Ground Zero was a challenge due to the ever-changing environment, smoke and fire predominantly. US Army personnel with loaded weapons, multiple checkpoints and concern over the buildings' structural soundness all worked into the psyche of everyone involved."[55]

In the Morgue

In the makeshift morgue, the bone experts worked twelve-hour shifts, seven days a week, identifying and separating all the human remains that were pulled from the site. Because tissue adhered to most of the remains, the anthropologists had to be adept at identifying more than bones. Craig, who spent more than a month at the scene, explains her first responsibilities:

The skeletal remains of a murderer have been preserved for over 100 years in Haubey Museum, Rock Island, Illinois.

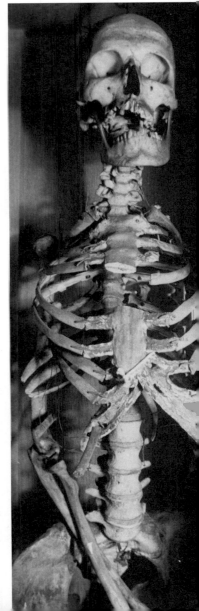

> If a bag came in filled with a twenty-pound mass of muscle, skin, and bone, we had to be able to tell either by feel or by sight if the tissues were connected. If a bone led to a tendon, and then to a muscle, and the other end of the same muscle was connected to yet another bone, then the entire specimen could stay together and be processed as a single set of remains. . . . But if we determined that there was no physical connection between one part and another, then we'd separate the remains and give them two different case numbers.[56]

Only rarely were remains found that led to immediate identification of a victim. When investigators found the tip of a finger, a small piece of skin with a distinctive tattoo, a gold-capped tooth, or an arm bearing a unique wristwatch, however, they knew there was a good possibility it could be identified using missing person reports or dental records.

Identifiable or not, every item was placed in a bag and passed on to pathologists, fingerprint experts, forensic dentists, and other specialists. DNA was also taken from each set of remains in hopes that victims could later be identified genetically.

Fresh Kills

Ground Zero was not the only site where forensic anthropologists practiced their special skills. At the enormous Fresh Kills landfill on Staten Island, they helped inspect some of the 1.8 million tons of debris that had been sorted and moved away from Ground Zero.

The process was tedious, as well as mentally and physically grueling. Working in twelve-hour shifts, examiners scanned debris on conveyer belts in the hopes of turning up traces of human tissue or personal effects that might have been missed during an earlier search. Nothing larger than a hand was ever found, but every scrap of tissue and bone was bagged and sent off for DNA identification. Anthropologist Michael Warren of the University of Florida states, "Our primary role was to examine all of the organic material and determine whether or not the tissue was human or non-human [such as remains of pets or meat from restaurants]. Non-human remains

Debris from the September 11, 2001, attack on the Twin Towers was brought to a landfill, where investigators searched for evidence, property, and remains of the victims.

would simply prolong the identification process and unnecessarily add to the tremendous expense of DNA testing."[57]

Despite everyone's hard work, as of September 2004, more than one thousand remains were still unidentified and had been stored in refrigerated trucks parked behind the New York City medical examiner's office. Plans were made to enshrine them as part of the World Trade Center Memorial that would be constructed beginning in 2006. "We're hoping that someday in the future, we might have the technology to identify those remains,"[58] says Ellen Borakova, a spokeswoman for the medical examiner's office. For the anthropologists who did all they could to match names and faces with those bits and pieces, that day cannot come too soon.

CHAPTER 5

Rebuilding the Bones

Forensic anthropologists not only are skilled at sorting bones, but many are able to rebuild faces from skulls in an effort to identify unknown victims, confirm identities, and reenergize cold cases. The three-dimensional images they create are a last resort when there are no witnesses or leads and the remains have not been matched to a missing person.

The process is considered a "best scientific guess" because it is impossible to know exactly how muscles and connective tissue once lay on a skull to make the victim's face unique. Still, with advanced technology, close approximations are becoming more feasible. Computer/forensic science expert Damien Schofield of the University of Nottingham in England says, "The Victorians were fond of sticking pins in corpses to measure tissue depths and, to be honest, that's all the data we had to go on till a few years ago. However, with CT [computer tomography] scans and MRI [magnetic resonance imaging], . . . we can now get better quality data samples and larger, more accurate data sets."[59]

Modeling Clay

The method most relied upon for three-dimensional facial reconstruction involves the use of markers and clay. The process begins with the skull. Markers that look like pencil erasers are cut to lengths that approximate the depth of the tissue at various points on the face. These depths were determined by researchers who carried out studies and compiled their findings. For instance, they found that tissue at one of the thickest parts of the face, the cheek, averages about 3/4 inch deep (19.5mm) in the average person of European ancestry. Tissue

This intricate forensic facial reconstruction of a shattered skull was made with clay.

Becoming a Forensic Artist

Job Description:

Forensic artists help identify victims or suspects using such disciplines as composite art, image modification, age progression, and postmortem reconstruction. Work is carried out in the studio. Hours are irregular.

Education:

Aspiring forensic artists must have a high school diploma. A bachelor's degree in criminal justice from a four-year college or university is recommended but not always required. Formal art training is usually required, and some agencies offer specialized forensic art courses. A portfolio of work is necessary to demonstrate artistic skills.

This forensic artist is adding detail to the reconstruction of a murder victim's head.

Qualifications:

Once their education is completed, forensic artists are encouraged to achieve board certification through the International Association for Identification.

Salary:

$30,000 to $40,000 annually

at one of the thinnest spots on the face—where the nasal bone meets the cartilage on the bridge of the nose—averages about 1/10 inch (2.5mm) deep.

Once markers are cut to correct lengths, they are glued on at specific locations, including the forehead, cheekbones, and jaws. The length of the markers tells the reconstructionist how thick to make the clay that is laid over the face and skull. Once the strips of clay have been applied, the nose, lips, and other features are modeled. The reconstructionist again relies on standardized proportions that researchers have determined through years of research. For instance, the average nose has been found to be one-third wider than the nasal opening in the skull. The mouth is about as wide as the distance between the pupils of the eyes. The ears are roughly the length of the nose.

Reconstruction is not based simply on standardized proportions, however. Every person varies from the average in numerous ways, and the reconstructionist cannot know whether a victim's ears stuck out or lay flat to the head, whether the nose was pointed or bulbous at the end, or whether the eyelids drooped or one eyebrow was higher than the other. Those and many other details have to be left to the reconstructionist's interpretation, and may in the end differ dramatically from the victim's actual features. That is why reconstruction is not considered extremely accurate, even when done by the most skilled reconstructionist. Anthropologist Kathy Reichs recalls, "I had one case, I did a test. I had seven different facial approximations done by different people with different techniques. They were all different. So it's an art not a science."[60]

A Tissue Depth Database

In an effort to make facial reconstructions more precise, recent researchers reviewed the tissue depth studies and noted that most of them had been carried out on the dead. This, they believed, caused some of the measurements to be inaccurate. For instance, bodies dehydrate after death, and this could affect the thickness of the tissue and thus the look of the face. Early studies were also done primarily with older Caucasian males. Tissue depths for females and persons of other ethnicities were likely to be slightly different.

To gain more accurate data, researchers broadened the scope of earlier studies. They studied tissue depth according to ethnicity and weight. They took advantage of new technologies such as ultrasound to take measurements on living subjects. One study, done by the Forensic Anthropology and Computer Enhancement Services (FACES) lab at Louisiana State University in Baton Rouge, measured the tissue depths on faces of more than 250 adults and 500 children. Results showed that there were significant differences based not only on sex and

A partially reconstructed head is pictured alongside a completed one. The pegs indicate appropriate tissue depths.

ethnicity, but also on age. For instance, men showed an increase in tissue depth at all the midline facial points and the cheek points as they aged. Aging females showed increased tissue depth at all points except around the eyes, below the temples, and at the middle of the lower jaw.

Rapid Prototyping

Recent research has also addressed instances in which a skull cannot be used as a model for reconstruction. For example, a skull may be fragile due to fire, or it may bear knife

marks that need to be protected and preserved as evidence in a trial. To get around such obstacles, researchers turned to a new technology called rapid prototyping to produce a detailed three-dimensional likeness of the skull without harming it.

Rapid prototyping, also known as solid free-form fabrication or computer-automated manufacturing, first became available in the 1980s. The process involves a specialized machine that reads data from a three-dimensional computer-aided design drawing. The machine lays down thin layers of paper, liquid plastic, or powdered plastic that are glued or fused together. As one layer is laid on top of the other, the figure described in the drawing gradually takes shape.

Rapid prototyping was first used in forensics in the 1999 case of a woman whose body was found on the banks of a river near the town of Spring Green, Wisconsin. Most of the flesh had been cut from the bones. A few fingerprints remained, but did not match any records, and a lack of dental work made checking dental records useless. From the shape and condition of the bones, experts were able to determine only that the victim had been female, black, and about twenty-five years of age.

When the investigation stalled, law enforcement officials decided to try facial reconstruction. Knife marks on the skull meant it could not be used as a model, so three-dimensional

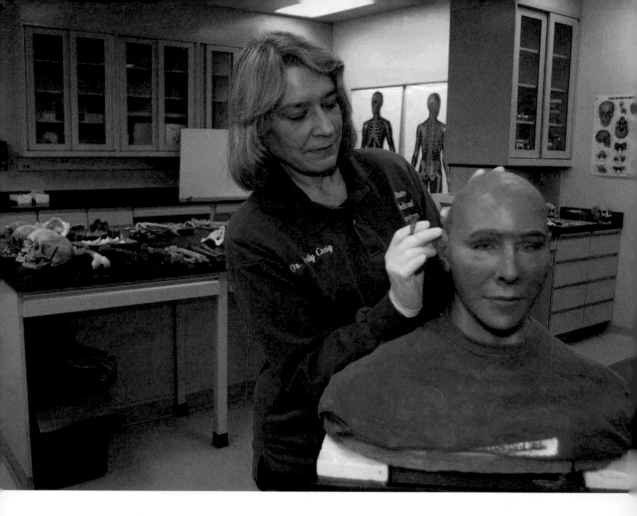

Forensic anthropologist Emily Craig works on a three-dimensional facial reconstruction to help identify an unknown murder victim

computer scans of it were taken to a rapid prototype center at the Milwaukee School of Engineering. There, an exact replica was created out of hundreds of layers of paper laminated with polyurethane resin.

The replica was then sent to Emily Craig, who used it to model a clay bust of the victim. When photos of the image were circulated around the state, the victim was identified as a Tanzanian student named Mwivano Mwambashi Kupaza. Craig says, "[Law enforcement] was then able to find a photograph of Mwivano, which resembled my reconstruction almost exactly. They went on to match the prints lifted from the remains . . . with fingerprints lifted from medical records that Mwivano had touched. . . . Finally we had our positive ID."[61] Kupaza's cousin was eventually charged with her murder, found guilty, and sentenced to life in prison.

Computer-Aided Reconstruction

In addition to their use in rapid prototyping, computers have proven invaluable to facial reconstructionists in other ways. In some labs, creating a computer-generated model of a victim has become a viable alternative to building a three-dimensional face out of clay. The skull is placed on a turntable and scanned by a laser, which feeds information into the computer. Using special software, that information is assembled into a basic three-dimensional likeness on the screen. Then the program is used to virtually apply tissue based on sex and ethnic origin. Blending tissue depth data makes it possible to accommodate victims with mixed racial ancestry. A library of facial features is available. The image can be morphed through different age progressions and adjusted for different weights, and it can be turned and viewed in a variety of lighting conditions. Martin Evison, a senior lecturer in forensic and biological anthropology at Sheffield College in England, says, "Instead of modeling muscles in clay we model them by computer, in virtual reality. The artistic skills are the same, but the artist works with a computer, keyboard, and tablet rather than with a bag of clay."[62]

"Baby Lollipops"

Forensic anthropologists who specialize in facial reconstructions do not limit their work to three-dimensional models to identify victims and help solve crimes. They also use their knowledge of facial structure and computers to make two-dimensional images more true to life.

Craig was one of the first to use computer enhancement when faced with an unidentified and almost worthless photo of a victim. In October 1990 the badly beaten remains of a child

By the Numbers

55%

Percentage of Americans who feel that the laws regarding the sale of firearms should be stricter in the United States.

Step by Step: Facial Reconstruction

Recreating the face of a victim takes patience and artistic skill. The reconstructionist proceeds as follows:

1 If a real skull is used, the lower jaw must be glued to the upper jaw to make it secure.

2 Tissue depth markers are glued to at least twenty-one specific locations on the face.

3 Measurements of the nasal opening, nasal spine (the bone that juts forward from the skull at the base of the nose), and gum lines are taken. These are used to help determine the size of the nose and mouth.

4 The skull is positioned on a stand. Cotton is placed in the eye orbits, nasal opening, and ear openings to prevent delicate bones from breaking during reconstruction.

5 Tape and then clay is applied to form a base for the eyeballs. Mannequin or prosthetic eyes are placed in the orbits, clay is used to fill in around them, and upper and lower eyelids are created from clay.

6 Strips of clay of the appropriate depth are used to connect the markers on the face and head. The space between the strips is then filled with clay to the correct depth.

7 The temples and cheeks are filled with clay to the depth indicated by the markers.

8 **For the nose,** a block of clay is cut to size using a formula based on the length of the nasal spine. The block is placed at the base of the nasal opening and over the nasal spine. This gives the projection and tilt of the nose. Balls of clay representing the nostrils are placed on each side of the block. The remaining portion of the nasal opening is filled in.

9 **For the mouth,** a block of clay is cut to size based on earlier measurement of the gum line. The block is placed over the teeth, reaching from canine tooth to canine tooth. Clay is filled in around the mouth to a depth appropriate for lips.

10 **The clay is smoothed** and molded to create a lifelike appearance. Appropriate age marks such as jowls and eye wrinkles are added as necessary. Ears, neck, and a wig are added.

11 **The reconstruction** is photographed. If a real skull was used, the clay is removed using warm water and a soft brush. Tissue depth markers are removed with acetone, which dissolves glue but does not harm bone.

An artist smoothes the clay on a forensic reconstruction of a head.

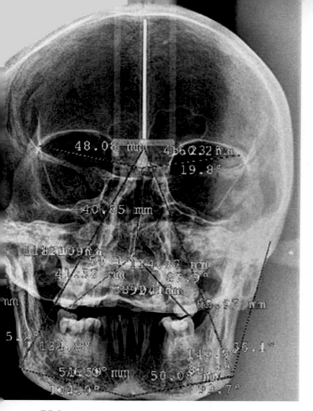

Using computer technology (above), forensic scientists created a reconstruction of a man (right) who lost his life in Pompeii during the eruption of Mt. Vesuvius in A.D. 79.

wearing a T-shirt with lollipops across the chest were found in Miami Beach. Because the wounds to his face made the child unrecognizable, Craig, who was a medical artist before becoming an anthropologist, was asked to recreate his face so that it could be circulated in newspapers for identification purposes. She writes, "The investigation couldn't proceed until the police knew who the child was. Because the crime had been so brutal . . . photos of the child's battered, bruised, and swollen body [could] not be made public. Nevertheless, he needed a face."[63]

Craig set about her work by scanning the child's photo, along with a variety of children's facial features, into her computer. She then selected features that seemed to fit the child, cut them out digitally, and placed them over the features of "Baby Lollipops," as the press called him. She left his facial shape, hair, neck, and shoulders untouched. Finally, she blended and smoothed the features until the whole thing looked like the photo of a live little boy.

The results were successful. A former babysitter identified the child as three-year-old Lazaro Figueroa, and other respondents soon came forward to testify that his mother had repeatedly abused him. Craig explains, "Soon after my picture of Baby Lollipops was published, the police were deluged with calls, and by early December they found and arrested the child's mother."[64]

Missing Children

In addition to using computers to digitally erase wounds, anthropologists also use the machines to manipulate images to show how a person might look after a long period of time. The process is particularly useful in cases involving missing children, whose looks change dramatically as they grow older.

Age progression is carried out regularly at the FACES laboratory. Established in 1994, the lab is associated with the National Center for Missing and Exploited Children and is headed by Mary Manhein. She says, "For those children who enter our laboratory in boxes or in bags, there is no hope; for those who are missing and unaccounted for, hope drives us steadily, though warily, toward our goal—finding them alive. . . . Though all such searches do not have happy endings, some do."[65]

To age a child's face, technicians at the FACES lab need a photo of the child at the age he or she went missing. A photo of a parent or sibling whom the child resembles, depicting him or her at the age the missing child would be in the present, is also vital. The photos are scanned into a computer and, using software designed for the purpose, slowly merged. The process causes the child's face to mature in ways that match the parent's or sibling's. The face lengthens and the cheekbones become more prominent. The eyes narrow. The mouth widens, and the nose grows longer. Light-colored hair darkens.

To complete the look, technicians add features such as up-to-date hairstyles and clothing from databases. The resulting image might not be an exact depiction of the child at an older age, but is often close enough to rekindle public interest and generate new leads when it is published.

Faces of Fugitives

Age progression is also useful in updating faces of long-term fugitives, whose appearance inevitably changes as they grow older. To carry out this procedure, technicians begin with a photo of the subject's face at the age he or she disappeared. Retaining the basic features that are generally the same throughout life, such as the smile and the expression around the eyes, they manipulate the photo, taking into account that most faces age a certain way. Upper eyelids generally droop, for instance, and pouches or circles appear under the eyes. Lips become thinner. Lines that are almost unnoticeable in early years become deeper. Skin on the neck sags. In men, hair often thins and eyebrows grow thicker.

If possible, technicians also draw on knowledge of how the subject's family members have aged and how the subject's personal habits may have affected the present look. For instance, if the subject is known to have been a heavy smoker, the technician will wrinkle and age the skin accordingly. Forensic artist Karen T. Taylor says, "If someone is a health nut, he will age one way versus the way a drug abuser or someone with thyroid condition will age. Our health is reflected in our faces."[66]

Technicians at the FACES laboratory were able to help bring at least one fugitive to justice using age progression. In 1997 the FBI asked the lab to age enhance a twenty-year-old photo of Thomas Gordon Jones, a suspect in the 1973 murder of former Louisiana state senator H. Alva Brumfield. After more than two decades, Jones was located in Texas, where he had been living under an assumed name. Investigators had obtained his current driver's license photo, but Jones had aged, and they wanted to be sure he was the correct man before arresting him.

The photo of the younger Jones was age progressed, and when it was compared to the license, the resemblance was marked enough for an arrest to be made. Jones was found guilty of the murder and received a ninety-nine-year sentence.

Photographic Superimposition

Forensic anthropologists use another computer technique, known as photographic superimposition, to confirm suspicions that a skull is that of a killer or a murder victim.

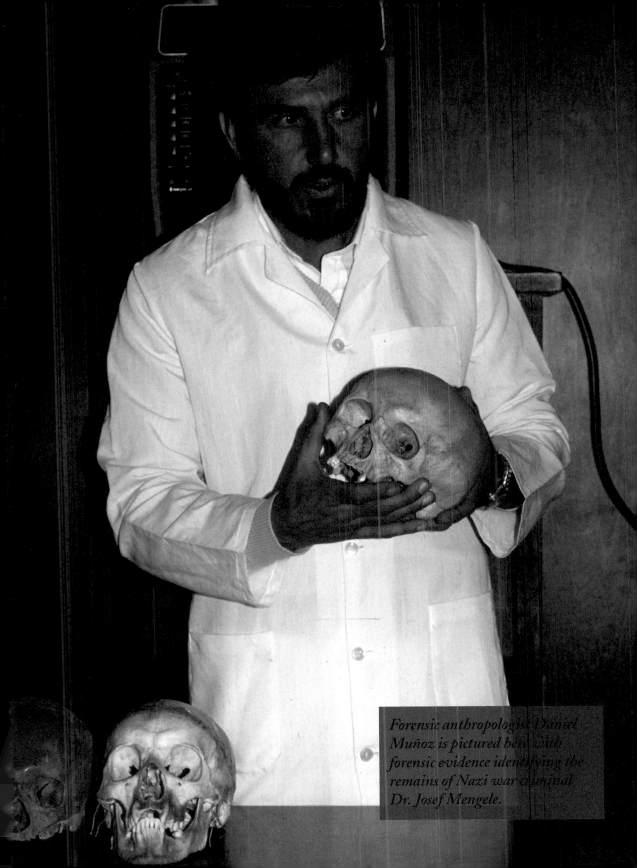

Forensic anthropologist Daniel Muñoz is pictured here with forensic evidence identifying the remains of Nazi war criminal Dr. Josef Mengele.

To carry out photographic superimposition, the remains must be of an adult, and examiners must think they know the identity of the remains. They must also have a photo of that individual's face to match to the skull. The process is based on the fact that skulls vary greatly in shape from person to person. Some are narrow and some are round. Eye sockets differ in size, shape, and placement, as do nasal openings. With such variations in mind, examiners begin by digitizing the photo and the skull in question. Adjustments are made so both are the same size and are viewed from the same angle. Using a software program, the face is superimposed over the skull and the image is manipulated so the skull appears visible through the skin.

Then a careful comparison is made to see if certain points—such as the top of the head, chin, eye sockets, cheekbones, nasal opening, and teeth—line up. If there are obvious differences—for instance, if the eyes in the photo do not lie squarely in the eye sockets of the skull—an exclusion is made. Every point must match exactly for a positive identification. Examiners are especially pleased if they can find a unique feature, such as a scar that sits directly over a healed fracture in the bone, to cement the determination.

One of the most celebrated cases of photographic superimposition involved the identification of Josef Mengele, a Nazi doctor known as "The Angel of Death" because he supervised the murder of more than four hundred thousand Jews in Europe during World War II. When the war ended, Mengele fled to South America, where he lived in seclusion under the name Wolfgang Gerhard. He was believed to have died by drowning in 1979.

American, German, and Jewish Nazi hunters had tracked Mengele for decades, but never caught him. When the Nazi leader's alleged death in Brazil was announced in 1985, all wanted to authenticate the skeletonized remains. Clyde Snow and German forensic anthropologist Richard Helmer were two of the experts called in to carry out the examination.

Reconstructing Bach

One of the pioneers of facial reconstruction was Swiss anatomist Wilhelm His, who in 1895 set out to prove that an individual's face could be reconstructed from nothing but his or her skull. His first took measurements of the tissue depths of twenty-eight male and female corpses by sticking an oiled sewing needle into the flesh of their faces at various points. When the needle hit bone, His marked the depth with a rubber disk on the needle's shaft. His recorded the depth to which the needle sank at each position, noting that at corresponding

Swiss anatomist Wilhelm His identified the skull of Johann Sebastian Bach (pictured above) using early reconstruction techniques.

points such as the upper lip and the temple, the thickness of the tissue was much the same from person to person.

His compiled this information into a table that became the basis for the measurements used in facial reconstruction today. He also used the information he gathered to prove that a skull believed to be that of Johann Sebastian Bach was indeed that of the renowned composer. Using the numbers he had collected, His commissioned an artist to create a face from the skull. The finished product bore a close resemblance to portraits of Bach made during his lifetime, proving that the technique could be used to provide a recognizable image of a real person.

A visual inspection of the bones confirmed they had belonged to a male of Mengele's size and age, but there were other men in the world who fell into that category, too. Thus, Snow and Helmer turned to photographic superimposition using the skull and a photo of Mengele taken during the war. When the two images were aligned, all points of comparison matched. Helmer told the audience of scientists that gathered in his lab to see the superimposition, "This isn't fantasy. This is Josef Mengele."[67] A year later, DNA analysis verified Snow and Helmer's findings—the remains were indeed those of Mengele.

Using a computerized image of a skull unearthed in Chile, forensic experts hope to identify an anonymous victim of genocide.

Looking to the Future

The use of photographic superimposition is likely to diminish as molecular approaches such as DNA analysis become increasingly available to forensic anthropologists in the future.

Computers and other high-tech equipment will also provide new tools to enhance their expertise at reading the bones. With the world's growing appreciation of their talents, they are thus likely to play an increasingly important role in helping law enforcement solve forensic cases as time passes.

The new opportunities suit them perfectly, not because they crave the spotlight, but because of the obligation they feel to better understand and aid the silent victims with whom they work. As William Maples wrote before his death in 1997: "[Skeletons] have tales to tell us, even though they are dead. It is up to me, the forensic anthropologist, to catch their mute cries and whispers, and to interpret them for the living, as long as I am able."[68]

Notes

Introduction: The Bone Experts

1. Quoted in Kelley Reese, "Death Defying," University of North Texas News Service, January 22, 2004. http://web2.unt.edu/news/story.cfm?story=8767.

2. Quoted in Christopher Joyce and Eric Stover, *Witnesses from the Grave: The Stories Bones Tell.* Boston: Little, Brown, 1991, p. 217.

3. Emily Craig, *Teasing Secrets from the Dead: My Investigations of America's Most Infamous Crime Scenes.* New York: Crown, 2004, p. 46.

4. Mary H. Manhein, *The Bone Lady: Life as a Forensic Anthropologist.* Baton Rouge: Louisiana State University Press, 1999, p. 9.

Chapter One: Recovering the Bones

5. Douglas Ubelaker and Henry Scammell, *Bones: A Forensic Detective's Casebook.* New York: HarperCollins, 1992, p. 27.

6. Quoted in Carlton Stowers, "Haunted House," *Dallas Observer,* November 27, 2003. www.dallasobserver.com/issues/2003-11-27/news/feature_5.html.

7. Manhein, *The Bone Lady,* p. 38.

8. Bill Bass and Jon Jefferson, *Death's Acre: Inside the Legendary Forensic Lab the Body Farm Where the Dead Do Tell Tales.* New York: Putnam, 2003, p. 78.

9. Bass and Jefferson, *Death's Acre,* p. 73.

10. Quoted in Bass and Jefferson, *Death's Acre,* p. 74.

11. Craig, *Teasing Secrets from the Dead,* p. 139.

12. Manhein, *The Bone Lady,* p. 58.

13. Bass and Jefferson, *Death's Acre,* p. 228.

14. Roxana Ferllini, *Silent Witness.* Willowdale, Ontario: Firefly, 2002, p. 82.

15. Bass and Jefferson, *Death's Acre,* p. 95.

16. Bass and Jefferson, *Death's Acre,* p. 95.

17. William R. Maples and Michael Browning, *Dead Men Do Tell Tales.* New York: Doubleday, 1994, p. 45.

Chapter Two: Reading the Bones

18. David Fisher, *Hard Evidence: How Detectives Inside the FBI's Sci-Crime Lab Have Helped Solve America's Toughest*

Cases. New York: Simon & Schuster, 1995, p. 12.

19. Bass and Jefferson, *Death's Acre*, pp. 40–41.

20. Bass and Jefferson, *Death's Acre*, p. 35.

21. Bass and Jefferson, *Death's Acre*, p. 101.

22. Craig, *Teasing Secrets from the Dead*, p. 56.

23. Ubelaker and Scammell, *Bones*, p. 102.

24. Bass and Jefferson, *Death's Acre*, p. 40.

25. Craig, *Teasing Secrets from the Dead*, p. 101.

26. Craig, *Teasing Secrets from the Dead*, p. 200.

27. Maples and Browning, *Dead Men Do Tell Tales*, p. 33.

Chapter Three: Broken Bones

28. Maples and Browning, *Dead Men Do Tell Tales*, p. 2.

29. Ubelaker and Scammell, *Bones*, p. 214.

30. Ubelaker and Scammell, *Bones*, p. 246.

31. Ubelaker and Scammell, *Bones*, p. 115.

32. Craig, *Teasing Secrets from the Dead*, p. 134.

33. Maples and Browning, *Dead Men Do Tell Tales*, p. 63.

34. Maples and Browning, *Dead Men Do Tell Tales*, p. 65.

35. Craig, *Teasing Secrets from the Dead*, p. 134.

36. Bass and Jefferson, *Death's Acre*, p. 190.

37. Ubelaker and Scammell, *Bones*, p. 193.

38. Maples and Browning, *Dead Men Do Tell Tales*, p. 171.

39. Craig, *Teasing Secrets from the Dead*, p. 135.

40. Maples and Browning, *Dead Men Do Tell Tales*, p. 178.

41. Craig, *Teasing Secrets from the Dead*, p. 226.

42. Craig, *Teasing Secrets from the Dead*, p. 226.

Chapter Four: Sorting the Bones

43. Quoted in Joyce and Stover, *Witnesses from the Grave*, p. 217.

44. Quoted in Joyce and Stover, *Witnesses from the Grave*, p. 248.

45. Quoted in Joyce and Stover, *Witnesses from the Grave*, p. 268.

46. Quoted in Rachael Post, "When the Bones Speak Out," Center for Latin American Studies, University of California, Berkeley, November 17, 2000. www.clas.berkeley.edu:7001/Events/fall2000/11-17-00-snow.

47. Quoted in Post, "When the Bones Speak Out."

48. Quoted in Jon Alter, "My Kind of Town," *Harvard Crimson*, January 9, 1979. www.thecrimson.com/article.aspx?ref=159596.

49. Joyce and Stover, *Witnesses from the Grave*, p. 108.

50. Joyce and Stover, *Witnesses from the Grave*, p. 123.

51. Craig, *Teasing Secrets from the Dead*, p. 249.

52. Craig, *Teasing Secrets from the Dead*, pp. 100, 112.

53. Craig, *Teasing Secrets from the Dead*, p. 236.

54. Craig, *Teasing Secrets from the Dead*, p. 239.

55. Quoted in Patrick Hughes, "CLAS Anthropologists Mobilized to NYC," *Alumni CLASnotes*, University of Florida, Fall 2001. http://clasnews.clas. ufl.edu/ news/alumninotes/01fall/nyc.html.

56. Craig, *Teasing Secrets from the Dead*, pp. 255–56.

57. Quoted in Joseph Kays, "The Human Toll," *Explore*, University of Florida, Spring 2002. http://rgp.ufl.edu/publi cations/explore/v07n1/terror.htm.

58. Quoted in Mike Kelly, "Ground Zero Memorial Plans Finally Right a Wrong," North Jersey.com, January 15, 2004. www.northjersey.com/page.php?qstr=eX Jpcnk3ZjczN2Y3dnFlZUVFeXky NjMmZmdiZWw3Zjd2cWVIRUV5e TY0NzU20DMmeXJpcnk3ZjcxN2Y3d nFlZUVFeXk5.

Chapter Five: Rebuilding the Bones

59. Quoted in *Vision*, "The Future of Forensics," University of Nottingham, 2005. http://research.nottingham.ac.uk/ Vision/display.aspx?id=807&pid=178.

60. Quoted in HBO.com, "Forensic Features: Q & A with Kathy Reichs," 2005. www.hbo.com/autopsy/forensic/qa_ with_kathy_reichs.html.

61. Craig, *Teasing Secrets from the Dead*, p. 209.

62. Quoted in Matt Bean, "Making John and Jane Doe's Faces More Familiar," CourtTV.com, July 30, 2003. www. courttv.com/news/2003/0718/does ketches_ctv.html.

63. Craig, *Teasing Secrets from the Dead*, p. 38.

64. Craig, *Teasing Secrets from the Dead*, p. 41.

65. Manhein, *The Bone Lady*, p. 67.

66. Quoted in Katherine Ramsland, "Computer-Altered Photography: Catching Fugitives," CrimeLibrary.com, 2005. www.crimelibrary.com/criminal_ mind/forensics/art/7.html?sect=21.

67. Quoted in Joyce and Stover, *Witnesses from the Grave*, p. 196.

68. Maples and Browning, *Dead Men Do Tell Tales*, p. 280.

For Further Reading

Books

Bill Bass and Jon Jefferson, *Death's Acre: Inside the Legendary Forensic Lab the Body Farm Where the Dead Do Tell Tales*. New York: Putnam, 2003. With coauthor Jon Jefferson, legendary forensic anthropologist Bill Bass tells his life story, including some of his most fascinating cases and his decision to create the Body Farm.

Blythe Camenson, *Opportunities in Forensic Science Careers*. Chicago: VGM Career Books, 2001. Offering information about a variety of careers within the field of forensics, this book includes training and education requirements, salary statistics, and professional and Internet resources.

Emily Craig, *Teasing Secrets from the Dead: My Investigations at America's Most Infamous Crime Scenes*. New York: Crown, 2004. Craig writes of her decision to become a forensic anthropologist as well as her many investigations of crime scenes throughout the United States.

Rexana Ferllini, *Silent Witness*. Willowdale, Ontario: Firefly, 2002. The book relates some of the techniques anthropologists use to identify human remains and help solve crimes. Includes case histories and interesting photos.

Donna M. Jackson, *The Bone Detectives: How Forensic Anthropologists Solve Crimes and Uncover Mysteries of the Dead*. Boston: Little, Brown, 1996. A brief but interesting look at the work of forensic anthropologists. Includes case studies and great photos.

Mary H. Manhein, *The Bone Lady: Life as a Forensic Anthropologist*. Baton Rouge: Louisiana State University Press, 1999. The director of the FACES laboratory shares many of her experiences as a forensic anthropologist.

William R. Maples and Michael Browning, *Dead Men Do Tell Tales*. New York: Doubleday, 1994. With coauthor Michael Browning, renowned anthropologist William Maples recalls his strangest, most interesting, and most horrifying investigations.

Peggy Thomas, *Talking Bones: The Science of Forensic Anthropology*. New York: Facts On File, 1995. Gives a complete overview of forensic anthropology. Includes actual forensic cases.

Katherine M. Ramsland, *The Forensic Science of CSI*. New York: Berkeley, 2001. Explores the forensic science used in the television series *CSI: Crime Scene Investigation*.

Douglas Ubelaker and Henry Scammell, *Bones: A Forensic Detective's Casebook*.

New York: HarperCollins, 1992. With coauthor Henry Scammell, the Smithsonian bone expert Douglas Ubelaker relates how he and his colleagues work with law enforcement to help solve murders.

Internet Sources

HBO.com, "Forensic Features: Q & A with Kathy Reichs," 2005. www.hbo.com/autopsy/forensic/qa_with_kathy_reichs.html.

Rachael Post, "When the Bones Speak Out," Center for Latin American Studies, University of California, Berkeley, November 17, 2000. www.clas.berkeley.edu:7001/Events/fall2000/11-17-00-snow.

Vision "The Future of Forensics," University of Nottingham, 2005. http://research.nottingham.ac.uk/Vision/display.aspx?id=807&pid=178.

Web Sites

Crime Library, Court TV (www. crimelibrary.com/index.html). A collection of more than six hundred nonfiction feature stories by prominent writers on major crimes, criminals, trials, forensics, and criminal profiling.

Disaster Mortuary Operational Response Teams (www.dmort.org/). This Web site provides a wide variety of information, including the history of DMORT, areas of service, team members, accomplishments, newsletters, and how to apply.

FACES Laboratory, Louisiana State University (www.lsu.edu/faces lab/). This Web site gives information about the lab, forensic anthropology, and victims that have yet to be identified.

Index

Picture Credits

About the Author

Diane Yancey lives in the Pacific Northwest with her husband, Michael, their dog, Gelato, and their cats, Lily and Newton. She has written more than twenty-five books for middle-grade and high school readers, including *Spies*, *Al Capone*, and *Life on the Pony Express*.